KICKIN' ROCKS

A ROMANCE

MARIANNE K. MARTIN

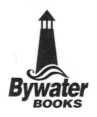

Bywater
BOOKS

Ann Arbor
2019

Bywater Books

Print ISBN: 978-1-61294-153-0

Bywater Books First Edition: July 2019

Printed in the United States of America on acid-free paper.

Cover designer: Ann McMan, TreeHouse Studio

Bywater Books
PO Box 3671
Ann Arbor MI 48106-3671
www.bywaterbooks.com

Always for Jo.

And for Maury Guilfoil,
who made people laugh when they wanted to cry,
and who left us way too soon.

Chapter One

2017

There was a lot Jada Baker didn't like about her neighbor, Buck Hodgins, and at the top of the list was how he treated his dog. Every day when she looked out her kitchen window, every day when she came home from work, every day she saw how he treated her—the heavy chain, the lack of shelter, the empty water bowl, dry dog food dumped over in the dirt. And today Jada's daily worry was wound so tightly on her chain that she couldn't sit up. Grateful for Sunday and not having to worry about being late to work, Jada slipped into untied sneakers and rushed out the back door.

It had all started the day Smokey got his name, the irrepressible need to help, to hear the cries of the innocent. It wasn't an obsession, a driving force that won't allow sleep until it's satisfied, at least not then. It was just the need of a ten-year-old girl to find her new kitten, to follow his cries until she and her father found that he had fallen down the fireplace shaft. They had saved him, lowered the end of a blanket until he caught hold, then pulled the tiny ball of ash-covered black fur to safety, and that's when it started. Now she couldn't turn away, or ignore the cries that kept her awake at night.

Jada called her Sweetness, sweet girl, sweet pie, and just Sweet. Because she was. And because the only thing the neanderthal who owned her called her was "Fuckstick." To him the only reason she was there was for protection, for his "business" or his hide. She was chained day and night to the framing plate of the house beside the door. The brown and white pit mix begin to whine and wiggle from front to tail the moment she saw Jada.

"Oh, I know, sweet girl, I'm coming." Jada unhooked the loose chain-link fabric from the bent fence rail and ducked through to the neighbor's yard. No pickup truck out front this early in the morning meant Buck had not come home last night. Nothing new, and it wouldn't have changed the situation if he had.

The dog's whine was at desperation level as Jada tried to find the quickest way to release the tight layers of chain wound tightly around her neck. "Okay, sweet girl, I know." Jada tried to work her fingers under the layers of chain to release it from the collar, but it was impossible. She turned her attention to the attachment to the house. Short of bolt cutters there was no releasing it where the heavy chain was welded to an eye bolt the size of a golf ball. There was no other way than to unwind, which meant that Sweetness had to cooperate.

Jada sat on the edge of a large crater that Sweetness had created in the dirt and wrapped her arms around the struggling dog. "Shh, shh. You have to calm down now or this isn't going to work. No," she said in a soft, low tone, "stop pulling and settle down." She continued speaking softly and stroking the strong shoulder and chest muscles until the raspy breaths eased and Sweetness finally relaxed on her side. After a minute or so of keeping her calm, Jada began to slowly pull the dog's upper torso clockwise toward the house. Little by little, half a turn in the moon crater, and the top layer of chain begin to loosen. Then with another turn Jada was able to take hold of the chain and began unwrapping it from the dog's neck.

When the last of the chain was unwound, the appreciation was immediate. In one quick move Jada was on her back in the center of the crater with sixty pounds of grateful dog wiggling on top of her and lavishing her with wet full-face kisses. Unmatched, unconditional. So immediate and clear, there was no appreciation like it. And for Jada the joy that came from it was as good as chocolate cake for breakfast or an extra vacation day.

But a moment later the rumble of a truck engine brought joy to the thin edge of anger. Jada managed to stand up, but as soon as she was upright Sweetness wrapped her front legs around her waist and clung tightly. Before Jada could dislodge herself, a six foot four, 290-pound hulk loomed uncomfortably close.

"She had the chain wound so tightly around her neck," Jada began," I was worried—"

"Stupid mutt," he growled, "ain't got the brains of a gnat." He slapped the top of the dog's head hard, adding, "Get down off her."

"She's fine," Jada replied. "I don't mind. She's a good dog."

"You go coddling her, girl, and she'll be even more worthless than she is now."

The need to hug the now cowering dog tugged against the fear of pushing the edge of the safety zone. Buck's physical presence would be enough for caution even without the stories. But the stories could not be taken lightly. After all, hadn't a bar full of people watched him stab a woman after a shouting match? Hadn't the mailman witnessed him beat a man into a coma in the post office parking lot for taking a parking spot he wanted? And every neighbor Jada knew suspected that his frequent five- and ten-minute visitors meant drug sales.

3

So, silence and a dared caress to the dog's head would have to suffice. Fear, or more aptly a healthy will to survive, won out today.

Sweetness. She was in Jada's head all day, from the beginning of her FedEx route to the end. Most of the dogs on her route brightened her otherwise stressful days, but they also reminded her that one sweet dog didn't enjoy the kind of life that most of them did. No loving home with hugs and treats and a comfy bed. No security against being hit or kicked, no one to protect against daily doses of vulgarities. Sweetness might not understand the words, but the meanness of their tone left its mark. Her saving grace was a bark that could alert even the hard of hearing and stop visitors well short of the door.

Throughout her day, Jada hurried between stops to allow time to refill Jacko's water pail, to give little Gracie half of her apple. The wiggles and excitement were many times more of a welcome than their humans signing for the packages. Today she had a delivery for Petie's mom. The truck lumbered up the sloping drive and stopped in front of the garage. Before Jada could retrieve the package and a special treat, the black and white border collie was standing on his hind legs outside the driver's door.

"Petie, Petie, my pretty boy," she exclaimed as she slid open the door.

He danced in a circle, then trotted alongside her as she carried the package to the door.

Mary Conner, recently divorced, waited on the porch. "Well, I have to tell you," she said, "I have been as anxious as Petie to see you. He can hear your truck a mile down the road and he comes to get me wherever I am."

"He knows that I always have something for him, too."

"This," Mary said taking the package, "is my new beginning. My online store is live tomorrow. Hopefully you will be picking *up* more packages from me now than you'll be delivering."

"Oh, I hope so." Jada smiled at Petie as he began his repertoire of tricks. "I'm going to have to carry a good stock of his favorite chicken strips." Petie lay down, backed up, rolled over, and sat with one paw up for a high five. "If I didn't give him a treat now, he'd do them all over again, wouldn't he?"

"And again, and again," Mary replied. "My ex used to make him go through them all two or three times, and then he would eat the treat himself. I had to get rid of him," Mary added with a laugh, "before he gave Petie a nervous breakdown."

"Aw, Petie, you get two today," Jada said, giving one strip to the waiting dog and one to Mary for later. "I have to get going, but I am so happy for you and excited to see your website tomorrow."

It had been a good day, filled with positives, and she left work with more than her usual anticipation to check on one sweet dog.

Two blocks from the house it was clear that the decision to go home before errands was the right one. Sweetness was racing through one yard and into another, hell-bent on her grand escape. Jada pulled to the side of the pavement and bolted from the car. She ran toward a side street, cutting the angle, trying to get in front of the dog to get her attention. And it worked. As soon as Sweetness saw her, she jutted toward her and bore down hard. Jada braced herself as sixty pounds of excited dog jumped on her. The bracing, however, proved inadequate, and Jada was quickly pinned on her back with Sweetness splayed on top, front paws on the ground on either side of her head.

"Okay, okay," she said, unable to avoid persistent wet kisses. She grabbed hold of the muscular neck and pulled Sweetness onto her side, then struggled to her feet." Come on, let's go for a ride." With the absence of a collar, Jada gripped the scruff of the dog's neck and escorted her to the car. There was no need to coax her into the backseat, but coaxing was necessary to get her out of the car and back into her yard. A couple of treats later Sweetness was once again hooked to the chain and her collar fastened through an unbroken hole in the leather.

"I'm so sorry, sweet girl. I wish I didn't have to do this to you." Jada hugged the dog's neck and kissed her head. "At least we got you back home before your neanderthal found out. He never has to know."

She should stay, play tug-o-war, spend some time with her, delay the whines that called and pleaded. But she couldn't. Buck would be home soon, and being in his yard, coddling his dog, felt at the least uncomfortable. So she would go do her grocery shopping, pick up a roasted chicken for dinner, and try to ignore the emotional tugging.

Jada wasn't fooling herself. It didn't take a master's degree to understand that it wasn't just the worry of a mistreated dog that stressed her. The impact that the political climate had made on her, and almost everyone she knew, was undeniable. What wasn't clear to her was how much focusing on something else, on the dogs on her route, on taking care of Sweetness, would actually help. As far back as she could remember, even as a young child it was the narrowing of her focus, the zeroing in on a singular, controllable matter that had always gotten her through the tough times.

When her mother was hit broadside by a driver running a red light, Jada had focused her energy and her fear on her mother's recovery. It was a full-out "head down, hands on, fix what she could" effort. She had monitored medications, asked a thousand questions. She had stayed up nights, pushed fluids and food, and dropped out of her college courses. It had been the only thing that she had control over. The only thing that seemed to ease the helplessness. Now, though, that method of coping, although tried and true for years, didn't seem to be enough.

Chapter Two

"It's a pain-in-the-ass rule," Jada muttered as she struggled to hold a large box with one arm and slide the truck door closed and lock it. "In the middle of the countryside, two miles between houses, and I need to safeguard cargo from thieves." A rule she admitted made sense most of the time. Today, though, it only frustrated her as she tried to make commitment times with so much ground between stops.

She carried the box to the little wooden shelter at the bottom of the long gravel drive and placed it inside. She was tired, sweaty, and hungry from fudging a lunch break in order to meet her numbers.

It had been a long day and all she wanted to do was gas the truck, clock out, and go home. But before she could unlock the truck door, noises from the brush next to the road caught her attention. She moved closer, listening carefully. There it was again, farther into the tall weeds. Soft, very young mews. Jada stepped cautiously where the ground dropped away into the weeds until she saw something white. When she separated the weeds, she found a pillowcase tied shut with a piece of rope. Jada picked it up and hurried back to the truck. Quickly she unlocked and opened the door, placed the bag on the seat, and tried untying the rope.

The mews were constant now. "I know, I know. I'm try-ing. Damn knot." She grabbed the box cutter and cut through the rope. Inside she counted five very young kit-tens, tiny balls of black and white and gray. "Oh, babies, sweet babies. How could anyone do this to you?"

There wasn't much she could tell about them except that they were too young to be weaned. How long had they been there? How long without nourishment? Would they be okay? Jada emptied her supply box, placed the pillowcase and the kittens inside, and set it between the seats. She knew exactly where to take them to find out.

The animal hospital, once a small family-owned practice, now occupied a sprawling new building on the north side of town. If she hurried, she could drop the kittens off there and make it back to the station without having to explain being late. But she could only push the speed limit once she cleared the township speed trap. A ticket wasn't an option.

Jada pulled into the parking lot and around to the side of the building to the emergency entrance. She and her box of babies were met inside by a young man. "Dr. Luca is on call," he said. "Let me get her."

The kittens were suspiciously quiet. She was stroking each little head gently, worrying that they seemed so weak and listless, when Dr. Luca swept into the room.

"Our FedEx lady," she said. "What do you have here?"

"Someone tied them in a pillowcase and threw them alongside the road. They seem so weak. I brought them right here as soon as I found them."

"Here, bring them back to the exam room and let's have a look."

Jada placed the box on the table, and the young man who had answered the emergency door joined the doctor. Jada quickly checked the time. Even if she left right now she would be late clocking in. She sent dispatch a short message—a monthly emergency, a woman's old standby excuse—then turned her attention to the doctor, who was lifting the kittens one at a time for a quick once-over.

"Are they going to be all right?"

"I'll do a more thorough check once we get some fluids in them." The doctor looked up as she answered.

Jada met her eyes—cocoa-colored directness, beautiful, concerned. She would take good care of the babies, that much Jada was sure of. "I have to get back to the station and clock out. Can I come back after that? To check on them?"

"Absolutely," Dr. Luca replied. "The front door will be locked, so come back to the emergency door," she said, backing toward the hall. "Let me get these little ones some help."

Jada thought of nothing else all the way to the station and back to the hospital, except whether the babies were going to be okay. She wanted to believe the best, to count on the care of Dr. Luca. So, in her mind she replaced the weak, shaky little cries with the confidence that she saw in the cocoa-colored eyes, and kept the vision right up until she was face to face with the doctor once again.

Concern registered on Jada's face. "How are they?"

"Lucky. At what I am guessing to be about two weeks old, I don't think they would have lasted another day out there."

Clearly relieved, Jada thought out loud. "Thank God for rules." She smiled and answered the questioning look from the doctor. "If I hadn't shut off the truck and locked the door, I never would have stopped long enough or been able to hear them."

The doctor nodded. "Well, I'm going to be honest, they

11

aren't home free. I'm hopeful, but . . . come on," she said, "let me show you what we're doing."

Jada followed her through the hall, past exam rooms to the back of the building where a large room was lined with walls of cages.

"We put them in the small room over here," Dr. Luca said, "so that it's easier to keep them warm." She crossed the room and knelt next to a small kennel covered with a blanket.

Jada knelt beside her as the doctor lifted the front of the blanket and opened the kennel door. The babies were cuddled together like pairs of rolled socks in the middle of a soft blanket.

"We'll keep them hydrated and warm on a heating pad," she said. "And we'll start them on formula every two hours while we try to find a nursing mother cat."

"What if you don't find one? Will they do okay on the formula?"

"This young, the absolute best for immunities and bonding is momma's milk. But second best is a rigorous feeding schedule and a lot of human contact, especially if these babies are feral."

"If it's okay," Jada said, "I'll come and help every day after work."

The doctor nodded. "I'm sure that will be fine."

"I'll still pay for their care, of course."

"Well," the doctor reached in and caressed each little ball of fur, "what are you thinking? Do you want to keep them or find homes for them?"

"My place is so tiny, I wouldn't have room for them. But I will take care of them until I can find homes for them."

"Okay, I'll see what I can do to help. We have a lot of contacts through the hospital here. First we'll see if we can find a momma to nurse them."

"Oh, I hope so. Thank you so much."

"That's what we do," Dr. Luca said, adding a smile. "Care for our fur babies."

The smile she offered was so genuine and so close—lightening the dark places, taking away, at least for a moment, Jada's uncertainty. It sparked a smile in return and the desire to see that smile for as long as possible. But the next moment the smile was gone.

"Josh is getting a feeding ready. Do you want to stay and help today?"

"Yes," Jada replied. "It will go a long way in helping me not worry so much."

"Then let's fill those little bellies."

Chapter Three

1966

"The purpose of NOW is to take action to bring women into full participation in the mainstream of American society now, exercising all the privileges and responsibilities thereof in truly equal partnership with men.... Further, with higher education increasingly essential in today's society, too few women are entering and finishing college or going on to graduate or professional school."

From T*he National Organization for Women's Statement of Purpose,* written by Betty Friedan, October 29, 1966

"It'll be approved. It *has* to be approved." Dusty Logan muttered the plea breathlessly in a half-run across campus. She shifted a heavy pile of books in order to glance at her watch. *Shit.* Dusty quickened her pace to its limit. It had taken two weeks to get a fifteen-minute appointment with the dean of Financial Affairs and she would *not* be late.

Dusty rushed down the hall and stopped outside the dean's office, set her books on the chair next to the door, smoothed her hair, and retucked her blouse into the waistband of her skirt. She took a deep breath, picked up her books, and entered the office.

"Miss Logan?" The secretary asked.

"Yes," she replied, consciously trying to slow her breathing as the secretary notified the dean.

"You can go in, Miss Logan."

Dean Roberts made only brief eye contact, nodded an impersonal welcome and diverted his attention to papers on his desk as Dusty took the seat across from him.

"I've reviewed your application for financial assistance," he began, still focused on the papers. "I'm sorry, but you really don't qualify for assistance."

The words felt like a punch to Dusty's midsection. "Why?" she managed through the emotional bruising.

Maybe it was her tone of desperation that forced the dean's eyes to meet hers, but it was only momentary. He picked up one of the papers. "You answered here that both of your parents are alive and in the home."

"Yes," she replied, not understanding the implication.

"And your father is working full time, so if they want you to continue in school they have the means to help you."

"They don't think I need an education. They won't give me any money for school. I work three jobs on top of my classes, but it just isn't enough." She blinked back the formation of tears.

"Well, if it's still important once you're married, maybe you could take some night classes."

No, not then, not later. She stared, transfixed on the elusive eyes, waiting for the rest, for the answer. She couldn't move, wouldn't move until he offered the solution, the answer she so badly needed.

The dean cleared his throat, allowed his eyes to meet hers. There was a flicker of chance she thought she saw there, but . . . "There's nothing I can do," he said firmly. "I have people waiting from families that can't help them."

His tone said there would be no argument, nothing that would convince him. The rules didn't account for her, or her dream. A gray-haired man with elusive eyes had just judged what her life should be without knowing or caring who she was.

It was that realization that allowed the tears as Dusty hurried back across campus. What was left? To clean the dentist's office, and the professor's house, and that of Mr. Gardener, who had lost his wife. And at the end of the semester her roommates would go home, and unless she could find a room she could afford, she would be forced to do the same. Something she did not want to do. Moving back home meant losing her independence, surrendering her dreams, and suffering the expectations of others. It had been uncomfortable before, but it would be unbearable now. Not the path she had planned, but right now she had no answers for an alternative.

Two banks had already denied her a loan. Dusty knew this one was her last chance. She had avoided this one, hoping that she wouldn't have to rely on her parents' good credit. She wanted to do it on her own, but this bank held the mortgage on her family's home, her parents' savings and checking accounts, and the loan that was sending her brother to college.

As she sat across the desk from her last hope, acid roiled from her stomach to leave a caustic taste in her mouth. She tried to swallow it away. *Please,* she pleaded silently. *Please.*

She was so close, just two more semesters and she would have enough to apply for a veterinary assistant's position that could help her pay for the rest of the education needed for certification. All she needed was a grant to help with tuition and she could make it. The housecleaning jobs would have to take care of housing, food, and minimal essentials. Books she would continue to get from the library. A little help, that's all she needed.

Below bushy white brows, the loan officer studied the application on his desk and then shuffled quickly through a separate folder. "Well," he said finally, "we might be able to work something out with your father." The brows lifted and he made eye contact. "Maybe a consolidated loan to include the one he has now. He'll need to come in and talk with me."

The little glimmer of hope she had felt flickered and failed. Though she knew the answer, she tried once more. "I was hoping to be able to take out a loan on my own."

He cleared his throat and slipped the application into the folder. His face softened into a fatherly condescension. That expression was enough. It said, you are a naive little girl, you don't understand how everything works, and explaining it to you won't get you a loan. So she knew before he said it.

"Well, you see, in order for us to loan money we have to have assurance that it will be paid back. It's called collateral, something that's worth enough to satisfy the loan in case of forfeiture—a house, a car . . ."

Dusty stood before he finished. She couldn't manage a "thank you"; it seemed inappropriate. How many jobs she'd had, how much she had paid on her own, nothing on that application mattered.

He followed suit and stood. "You, uh, tell your father to come in and see me and we'll see what we can do."

Dusty turned to leave but couldn't resist one last shot, one that she knew would be fruitless but needed release nonetheless. "My father thinks that a college education for a woman is a waste of time and money." His lack of reaction was no surprise. "So don't expect a visit from him."

What was the cost of independence? And dreams, what were their costs? In dollars, Dusty had a pretty good idea. A very progressive home economics teacher had put her high school students through an economic study that laid out the costs of living on your own, of going to college, and of raising a family. Those costs were clear. But there had been no study on the cost of *losing* independence, of surrendering dreams.

With a surge of frustration, she pushed the bank door to its limit and marched out. Every stride now pounded home its definition—anger, an ineffective punishment to the concrete below. Anger at the futility, at the unfairness—anger at the loss.

A year short of her goal she would go home. She'd work whatever jobs she could and save as much money as possible while her dreams were on hold. Meanwhile, she would deal with the loss of the freedom that had become so important to her. And, once again, Dusty would have to be the dutiful daughter—follow expectations, fit the image of the good, the normal girl. At least appear to be. Early nights, pretend boyfriends, and hidden desires. Honesty would come at too high a premium.

Chapter Four

A natural worrier. Her mother said it, her sister said it, good friends had said it. Jada's a natural worrier, there's no denying it. She worries about her mother's care if her disability is cut. She worries about the growing hatred that she sees in the news every night, and about meeting projected delivery numbers each day and keeping her job. And she has always worried about animals that are mistreated. It's just her nature.

So it didn't matter how hot and humid the days were or how harried her efforts to meet deadlines, she would hurry home each day to check on Sweetness, and now for the past two weeks to continue on to the hospital to help care for the babies.

Some relief came when Dr. Luca found a nursing mother that she felt could nurse three more. That left what the doctor deemed to be the two strongest of the litter in the care of humans. And each day that Jada held them and fed them they became more and more like her girls. A string of possible names began winding their way through her thoughts as she headed home from work today, and Jada welcomed the distraction.

But the distraction ended the moment she pulled into her driveway. Across her tiny front yard she could see an empty chain on the other end of the fence. Sweetness was loose—again. Jada jumped from the car, quickly surveyed the neighbor's yard, then headed down the middle of the narrow street. She whistled and called and scanned the yards on either side of the street. Mostly small yards, mostly small houses, nestled close together so it was nearly impossible to see behind them.

She stopped at the second corner and called and watched the yards where she had found her before. No movement. She called again. Nothing.

"Dog, cat, or kid?" The voice turned Jada around to see a woman in a tan Blazer stopped on the other side of the street. "What are you looking for?"

"Oh." Jada crossed the street to talk with the woman with the nearly shoulder-length gray and blond hair. "My neighbor's dog got loose again. He's not home, and I have to find her before he *does* get home."

"Come on," the woman said, "get in and we'll circle the neighborhood. What's her name?"

Jada hurried to the other side of the car and got in. "She doesn't really have a name, unless you count Fuckstick, which is all I hear her owner call her. I just call her every kind of sweet—Sweet girl, Sweetie, Sweetness."

The woman drove slowly toward the next corner. "You call out your window and I'll call out mine."

The Blazer crept down the streets and around corners with no sight of Sweetness. "It's my fault," Jada said. "I can't stand that she's kept on a short chain with a choke collar. She kept getting out of her leather collar so he got mad and put the choke collar on her a few days ago. It'll kill her. So I reversed it yesterday and sure enough, she's loose again."

"Who does that?" The woman asked, pulling down another street.

"A six-foot neanderthal who scares the piss out of me.

But she is such a good dog, I just can't stand to see her mistreated."

"What kind of dog is she?"

"A pit mix, but—"

"I have no pit prejudice," the woman said with a smile. "Actually, I'd trust a pit before I'd trust a lot of people."

"I just hope we can find her," Jada added. "I'd wish for her to keep running and let some family take her in and love her, but because she's a pit she'd end up in a shelter and you know what her fate is there."

They continued around the other side of the neighborhood, calling and whistling and not seeing anything except people coming home from work and kids on skateboards defying all parental directions.

"I appreciate you stopping and taking so much time to help me."

"Well, you looked a little frantic and I couldn't just drive by."

They made the turn onto the opposite end of Jada's street and both women let out a few more loud, strong whistles.

"The little yellow house down there on the left is mine," Jada said. "You don't have to keep looking. I'll go ahead and walk through the—oh, there she is!"

Jada already had the door open before the car came to a stop. Seconds later she was approaching a narrow empty lot with branches and discarded furniture scattered among the weeds. Sweetness was curled up in the seat of an overstuffed chair with her head facing away and resting on the arm.

"Sweet girl," Jada called. "There's my Sweetness." The dog's ears shot up and her head turned sharply. "Come on, girl. Come on."

The car pulled closer as Jada braced for a bounding welcome. She managed to stay on her feet and wrap her arms around the thick, muscular neck as Sweetness hugged Jada's waist. "Yes, I know, you're a good girl. I know. I know."

"Will she get in the car?" the woman called.

"Oh, she loves car rides. She just doesn't like going home. Come on, girl," Jada said, turning toward the car and opening the back door. Sweetness obediently jumped into the backseat. "I think she was liking that comfy ol' chair." Jada slid into the front seat and added, "I should drag it down and put it in his yard for her."

"He doesn't bring her in the house, does he?"

Jada shook her head. "No. I put straw under the side of the house for her when the nights start getting cold." She turned her head to see the happy, smiling dog in the backseat as the car stopped in front of her house. "Thank you," she said. "I really appreciate your help."

She got out and circled around to the back door nearest the yard to let Sweetness out, but before she could open the door the car started moving forward. The woman leaned out the window and said, "Remember two things. You weren't home when she got loose, and you don't know where she is." Then, before Jada could respond, the car pulled away with Sweetness still sitting happily in the backseat.

"Hey," was Jada's weak and stunned response. Was this woman just driving away with someone else's dog? She stared after the car, watched the woman wave out the window and turn out of sight. What had just happened? Had she helped someone steal Sweetness?

The woman's words stayed with her all the way to the hospital. *You weren't home when she got loose, and you don't know where she is.* As much as she wanted them to make her feel better, they didn't. She didn't know what she felt. A guilty relief, a strange sense of loss? What? How many times had she wished that sweet dog a loving home? Was this what had happened, a wish come true?

Josh answered the emergency door as usual. "I'm sorry," Jada began. "Something I couldn't help."

"No worries at all," he replied. "Babies are fed, but they can always use more love."

"Is Dr. Luca still here?"

"She's gathering up her things. I'll let her know you're here. Go on back to the babies."

"You don't need to bother her. I've already held her up too long."

But he was on his way down the hall anyway, and by the time Jada knelt in front of the kennel, Dr. Luca breezed into the room and knelt beside her.

"They're getting so active," she said. "And eating like champs. All good signs." She picked up the other kitten and held it to her chest.

"I didn't mean to hold you up. I assumed that no one would answer the office phone if I called to explain."

"No, it would have gone to a recording. But, it's fine. I'm on my way to get dinner before heading home. I have no energy for cooking tonight."

"I meant to ask you, and I don't know why I haven't, but are you staying late on nights that you aren't scheduled just so I can help with the kittens?"

"It's only been this week, and an extra hour a day is not a problem. People with your level of compassion lift me up."

Jada kissed the gray ball of fur and let it nuzzle against her neck. "I wish I knew how to thank you."

"Josh and one of the other staff told me about how you waded through knee-high snow all the way from the road this year when the snow removal guy didn't show up on time. We just may be getting close to even."

"I consider it part of the job."

The doctor raised her eyebrows. "So, they pay you extra to work the rest of the day wet from the knees down?"

"I carry extra socks. I admit that I wasn't prepared for frozen pant legs, though."

"Then consider this part of *my* thank-you."

"Done," she said, giving the kitten one last kiss before returning her to the kennel.

"Have you reconsidered maybe keeping these two?"

Jada hadn't expected the question, partly because she hadn't answered her own yet. The realization had come and gone a number of times that it wouldn't be long before she would have to leave and not see them again. But she had pushed it away.

"It's going to be hard to walk away from them," the doctor added.

"You're reading my mind."

"No, just watching you hold them and care for them— and how they're making you smile right now."

"I'd have to come up with some names," Jada replied. "I couldn't keep calling them the twins."

Dr. Luca smiled. It was an open, happy smile that raised her cheeks and widened her eyes, beautiful caramel-colored eyes telling Jada that this was what the doctor had hoped for all along.

"No, you weren't reading my mind," Jada said. "You were silently *willing* that I keep them, weren't you?"

"I can't think of a better place for them than with the one that saved them."

"I sure had a lot of help. I still need to find a way to thank you."

"Okay, if you aren't going to let that go, then come eat dinner with me. I'd enjoy some company."

Jada caught herself about to decline when she realized that she didn't have to get right home. For the first time in a long time there was no Sweetness to check on, no one to worry about.

Her hesitation was obvious, causing the doctor to say, "It's okay if—"

"Oh, no, it's a nice idea. I just normally have to get right home, but . . . where were you planning to go?"

"You're sure? I totally understand if —"

Jada was shaking her head. "No, it's that my otherwise normal routine changed today. So it really is fine."

"Then how does The Family Kitchen sound?"

"Perfect."

The local family-owned restaurant was known for a home-made-style menu and a regular clientele. Loyal customers counted on good food at an affordable price and a hands-on owner who knew them by name.

Jada felt more at ease than she had expected. They were settled comfortably in an end booth, awaiting their orders and sipping drinks. "I can see why you like to come here. It's . . ." Jada searched for the right word, ". . . comfortable."

Dr. Luca nodded. "I like that they know me, and ask about my day. I've decided that I eat alone too much. A night out now and then with friends doesn't seem to be enough lately."

"I know that feeling. No matter how tired I am there are times when I would gladly drag myself back into the car to spend some time just talking with someone, face to face; phone calls and internet aren't the same thing."

"Exactly. And I seem to have lost my single friends to relationships and marriages, so their availability is pretty slim."

Jada thanked the waitress as she placed their meals on the table, and added, "My stomach just growled at the sight of this."

"A little comfort food will take care of that," the doctor said, adding a bit of a smile and motioning to Jada's plate. "Chicken and mashed potatoes qualify as comfort food. I'm a sucker for mac and cheese when I'm stressed, so I have to watch myself."

"Okay, I'm blaming this one on no lunch and Sweetness." Jada acknowledged the questioning look from the doctor. "Sweetness, or actually *no* Sweetness, is why I didn't have to go home as usual today." She hadn't planned on sharing the strange story. She hadn't even had time to sort it out herself, but there it was, tumbling out like spilled gumballs to someone whose opinion, Jada realized, was important to her. "So," she concluded, "there's no sweet dog to rush home to."

"Or to worry about. Unless you think the woman steals dogs to sell for experiments or fighting."

Her uneasiness hadn't yet settled in and certainly hadn't gone to the fear that the doctor just suggested. Jada revisited the woman's face—gentle folds above soft hazel eyes, concerned crease between her brows, soft lines at the corners of her mouth—there was no hint of hardness, or of deception. "No, I think she sincerely wanted to help. Maybe it was the suddenness of it, the lack of warning, or being an unknowing part of the decision."

"If you are right and that's true, then she made sure that you weren't complicit. She's either quick as a whip, like my grandmother used to say, or she's done it before."

Jada finished a bite and sipped her tea. "So, is either of those bad?"

"I don't know that I could condemn a spur-of-the-moment decision to give a dog a better life. And I hope that's what it was." The doctor hesitated a moment and then added, "My Tres, my awesome little three-legged poodle, was one of those choices for me. She was born with a deformed leg, and the owner couldn't breed her or sell her so he brought her in to be euthanized. The moment I picked her up and she nuzzled against my neck I knew I wouldn't do it. She is such a happy little soul."

"Then why am I feeling like this, like I'm off-balance or something?"

28

"How long have you been worrying about her and taking care of her?"

Jada thought back. Could it really be that long? "About two and a half years, I think." She nodded. "This December will be the third Christmas. I always get her a giant chew bone after I caught her gnawing on a brick."

"And you probably fed her and played with her. You adopted as much of her as you could. And now she's gone." Dr. Luca held eye contact. "What you're feeling is a loss."

Jada finished another bite and let the thought linger. She would look out her kitchen window tomorrow and see only a loose chain and an empty crater in the dirt. There would be no desperate whines, no grateful, wiggling excitement wrapping itself around her—no more Sweetness. She finally offered an absent nod.

"Even if she wasn't totally your dog, you had a lot invested in her, a lot of love and concern. It's a natural reaction, Jada."

Her voice held a tone of resolve. "She's going to be okay. I believe that. I can't be selfish, you know," she said, looking to the doctor for a confirming nod. "It's not about me. It's about a great dog having a chance at a better life."

"Exactly. And now you've been responsible for the kittens having a chance."

"Do you think we'll find homes for them? I took pictures and posted them at work. How soon will we need to know?"

"Momma cat should start weaning them soon. But they're in good care whatever time it takes. The lady who has them fosters animals with special needs or when the shelters are full, which is quite often, I'm afraid."

"So, we'll be weaning the twins soon, too?"

"Yes," she replied, and asked the passing waitress for a take-home box. "You are going to have two frisky babies with antics that'll challenge your loss of Sweetness. They come with a guarantee—to make you laugh."

"And that's a guarantee I can really use these days. Every

day it seems that something that I assumed was a guarantee is threatened."

"I have no doubt that I'd be a depressed mess if I couldn't count on my work and my family. I let my dad tell his tales of teenage delinquency that make me laugh, and every day I look into the eyes of the most loving creatures and I know I'm going to be all right."

Jada concentrated on the doctor's eyes, on their sureness and the positive lift at their corners. She was sure that her own didn't offer the same, as much as she wished they did. Wishing over reality never worked for her. What she felt had always been what others saw. Poker, even for fun, would be an act of futility. But she had nothing to hide, so it rarely mattered and often required little explanation. "We are going to be all right, aren't we?"

"That's what I tell myself when the music stops and the light goes off at night. Lately, though, I'm having to become more and more creative."

Jada confessed, "I've been trying not to watch the news, but it's like a compulsion. As awful as it makes me feel, I can't stop."

"Staring at the train wreck."

Jada nodded. "And hoping that the train would be righted and miraculously no one was hurt."

"I don't know how we right the train." The doctor looked pensive—a look Jada imagined preceded a diagnosis or a risky procedure. "You know Josh at the hospital." Jada nodded and Dr. Luca continued. "He's a Dreamer. He keeps me aware every day of how much in my life I've never doubted, never worried about. A couple of other staff and I are going to a resistance march in Lansing and we asked him to come with us. He said no, and that's when I realized how terrified he is. He's *afraid* to resist, afraid to be *seen*."

"I thought they were protected, that at least *they* wouldn't be deported."

The doctor waited until Jada's eyes were centered on her

own. She hesitated before saying, "We can't assume that anyone is safe right now. Women, minorities—gays."

The emphasis was barely noticeable, a nuance waiting for acknowledgment, easily overlooked if irrelevant. But, of course, it was relevant. "I've never been afraid to be who I am," Jada replied, "and I sure don't want to start now."

"*No one* should have to, that's why marching is so powerful. I never thought that I would ever need to feel that kind of unity with people I don't know. But I find myself wanting to have the comfort of that unity. Have you been to a march?"

Jada shook her head, and took the bill from the waitress before the doctor could object. "I've got this," she said. "It's at least a start to thank you for all you are doing for the kittens."

Dr. Luca held Jada's gaze, tilted her head slightly and replied, "Not necessary, but I appreciate it."

Yes, there was a lot that Jada appreciated, too, beyond the doctor's compassion and skills. Maybe a friendship, she thought, reminding herself that appreciation and physical attraction can come and go, and that relationships are sometimes mercifully elusive. She liked this woman a lot. And it was becoming clear that it wasn't just the twins that she would miss seeing every day. But for now, as they headed to their cars, today might have to be enough.

"There is a march next weekend," Dr. Luca said as she rounded the end of her car. "Would you like to go?"

"Yes," Jada replied. "I would."

"I think it will lift us up," she said over the roof of the car. "Oh, and you need to start calling me Amie."

Chapter Five

Ann Arbor, Michigan 1971

"This is no simple reform. It really is a revolution. Sex and race, because they are easy, visible differences, have been the primary ways of organizing human beings into superior and inferior groups, and into the cheap labor on which this system still depends. We are talking about a society in which there will be no roles other than those chosen, or those earned. We are really talking about humanism."

From *Address to the Women of America* at the founding of The Women's Political Caucus, Gloria Steinem, July 10, 1971

Yes, she had heard it correctly, heard it said right out loud in public—exactly what had challenged Dusty Logan's identity for as long as she could remember.

"We are not second-class citizens," the woman commanding attention on the steps of the Michigan Union declared. "When are we going to stop acting like it?"

Second class.

"Do you have a credit card of your own?"

No.

"Are you being paid as much as the man working next to you?"

Am I? Mutterings from women standing around her said that *they* were not.

The tone of this woman's voice, challenging and strong, held Dusty captive. "Have you been passed over for a position by a man less qualified than you?"

The women gathered at the base of the wide granite steps answered, their yeses escalating to shouts.

"Why?" The woman shouted back. "Why is that okay?"

"It's not!" came the multi-voice response.

"Then do something about it! Ask for what you deserve!"

The shouts said "yes"!

"*Demand* what you deserve!"

Now it was Dusty's own voice joining the shouts.

"Expect what you deserve! Expect equality." She paused for a moment, nodding at the shouts, her eyes piercing the crowd with determination. "Now, let's pass the ERA!" She raised her fist in the air and the chant began.

"ERA! ERA! ERA!"

Dusty chanted with the others, releasing something undefined until now, heavy and restricting. The bindings, exposed now for their presence in her own life, snapped. The comparison to a brother, two years her junior, was clear. Her long-smoldering discontent, justified. Their duties growing up—hers domestic, cooking, cleaning, laundry; his, washing the truck and mowing the lawn. Their restrictions—hers, an eleven o'clock curfew; his, none. Their expectations—hers, wait tables until marriage; his, go to college and prepare for a career. The inequality, at home and publicly, had been sucking the oxygen from her, stealing her potential, her power. That she knew.

She looked at the women's faces around her and saw what must be shining from her own. Realization. Confirmation. She drank it in until she was intoxicated. The strength of it surrounded her. No vulnerable parts of her

34

left exposed. She felt safe. Strong. Shoulder-to-shoulder strong. She could ask, expect, demand, stay there on their common path for as long as it took.

But the woman with the commanding voice and intense eyes was leaving the steps toward the door of the Union and the crowd was dispersing. Dusty touched the arm of the woman closest to her. "What's her name?" she asked, motioning toward the closing door.

"Ali Nichols," the woman replied. "She's wonderful, don't you think?"

"Yes," Dusty said, rushing up the stairs. "Yes, I do."

She pulled open the heavy wooden door and looked quickly in each direction, just catching a glimpse of the dark bob and fashionably untucked powder-blue shirt. Determined to catch her before she was swallowed by a bustling crowd of students, Dusty wedged and excused and made her way through until she was able to reach forward and touch the woman's shoulder.

"Ali?" she said, her voice surprisingly sure. "Ali, could I talk with you?" Determined and sure—until the woman turned.

"Oh, of course," was the reply as sky-blue eyes stopped Dusty's world.

"I," *breathe,* breathe *dammit,* "I'm Dusty." *Jesus, what's wrong with me?* "Dusty Logan. I heard your speech out there."

A nod that Dusty barely noticed, still locked in sky-blue and scarcely breathing. Ali answered as if the world was perfectly measured and straight on its axis—as if reason was in control. "I was just headed for Union coffee and a quick bite. Will you join me?"

Yes, yes, anywhere. "If I'm not imposing," she managed, positive that she hadn't blinked once and unsure if her legs still worked.

"Not at all. Let's see if we can grab a table."

Freed from the gaze that had stolen her control, Dusty

willed her legs to keep up and followed Ali through the quickly filling room to claim a small table.

"You keep the table," Ali directed, "and I'll get us coffee and bagels."

She was gone in the next breath, giving Dusty the time needed to settle her heart rate below pre-stroke level and to take enough deep breaths to stay lucid. But enough time to figure out such a reaction? Probably not.

Attraction, certainly. Physically Ali Nichols was striking—tall, slender, built like a swimmer. And the hints of personality and values were appealing as well. Yes, she was attracted to this woman, but attraction wasn't new to Dusty.

Suzie Grasso in the ninth grade was *new*—first experiment, first exploration. A year of "best friend" public deception was good preparation for the secret gay dating game that followed. *This*, though, whatever it was had caught her off guard.

It had been just enough time for thoughts to begin to wander and the busy sounds of the room to settle into normal around her. But it only took the sight of Ali Nichols approaching the table to send a shock of electricity that unsettled everything once again.

"I'm sorry," Ali began, as she placed a tray on the table, "I got stopped twice before I could get across the room. But I do want to answer their questions."

"No, you do—I mean I appreciate that you do. It's . . ." *Oh please don't sound like an idiot.* "It's what I want too . . ." *and to somehow sound coherent,* "answers, I mean." And now a smile, wide and bright, below sparkling blue, and Dusty lost what little concentration she had.

"I'll do my best, Dusty. It is Dusty, right?" Ali acknowledged a silent nod with another smile. "Ask away."

Oh yes, just snap your fingers, ignore that your mind has been turned to mush by your reaction to this woman and ask an intelligent question. "What can I do?" *Pitiful. Beyond pitiful.*

"Politically? Personally?" Ali asked.

Dusty finally managed a deep breath. "I think both."

"Good, because much of what you do politically will affect you personally." Ali tilted her head and maintained direct eye contact. "You have to vote. Number one, above all else."

"This election will be the first that I can vote for a president." Dusty offered a grin. "I'll vote for whoever opposes Nixon. That'll cancel out my father's vote."

Ali leaned forward for a sip of coffee. She frowned when she said, "It needs to be more than that. You need to know what you believe in and vote for what and who supports that."

"I know what I don't believe in." Her own expression matched Ali's seriousness. "Most of what my father believes."

The intense eyes contemplated her over another sip of coffee. "Well," Ali said, looking up with a smile, "We have that in common. And now that I speak out publicly, my father knows just how strongly I disagree with him. I have become quite an embarrassment."

An embarrassment? For what? For standing up for what was fair and right? A parent should be proud to have a daughter like that, so strong and confident, and beautiful. No, an embarrassment was having your daughter turn out to be worse than a feminist, to have her dash your dreams of walking her down the aisle, of a son-in-law to watch football games with, and grandkids to dote over. No, Dusty understood real embarrassment. "You're not an embarrassment."

Ali smiled. "Eat your bagel," she said, reaching for one. "You should start contacting your representatives and senators and encourage them to ratify the ERA. Explain how important it is to you, give them personal reasons. When we leave, pick up a flyer in the hall with their contact information."

Dusty nodded.

"Write them. Call their offices. It's important."

Another nod. "I can do that."

"The hardest thing you can do, though, is to talk about it—to people who don't understand it, who don't think it is important." Ali hesitated, her brow knitting into a frown. "To other *women* who think that by ratifying this law they will lose their *privileges* as women."

"*Privileges?* Like what?"

"Their right to be supported by their husbands, for one. That it would not allow them to be stay-at-home mothers and wives."

"But what about women who don't marry or who *want* careers? Why shouldn't they be treated equally?"

"Because that takes away from what they see as the traditional American family. And they are afraid it will eliminate the man-only draft and force women into battle."

"But—"

"I know. They also fear that it will support abortion rights, and pave the way for homosexuals to marry. They have a boatload of reasons to choose from to fight this. And they are."

"Do *you* think any of that will happen?"

"It will support abortion rights," Ali replied, "the rest, probably not. But they are afraid to claim their own power."

"And they would deny that power to other women."

Ali nodded. "And they have a well-organized opposition to do just that. That's why I said that talking to those who don't want it ratified or are unsure is the hardest thing to do."

"But that was a big crowd out there today. They were all excited and supportive. And you are so confident and sure."

"Campus crowds are pretty easy. Most are students and most are well informed. They're ready to act. You need to come to a big NOW rally and hear women like Gloria Steinem and Bella Abzug. That's when you will see opposition."

"I want to," Dusty said, her words ringing with commitment. "I want to do my part."

"Gloria Steinem's going to be in Lansing on the 11th and there will be a large group from this area going. You should come with us. And if you're serious, organizers meet every Sunday in the basement of Mother Earth Gifts. Everything is on the flyer, so don't forget to pick one up." She took a last sip of coffee and placed it on the tray. "Talk it up in your classes, too," she added. "We'll add as many buses as we need."

"I will spread the word," Dusty replied, placing her cup and napkin on the tray, "but I'm not a student—not anymore anyway."

"Ah." Ali's face brightened. "When did you graduate?"

"I didn't. I couldn't make enough money to keep going. I work at bookstore now so I don't have to live at home."

"Another strong feminist making it on her own." Ali reached her hand across the table. "Nice to meet you. I was pre-law. I'll continue if I can get a better-paying job."

"Me, too."

"Okay, so the 11th is a date?"

A date? No, no, the *date—of the rally. Shit, Dusty, take a breath.* "Lansing," she confirmed. "Yes, yes of course."

"Meantime," Ali added, rising from her chair, "why don't you join us at the bookstore Sunday?"

"I'll be there." *Anywhere, everywhere.*

"It was nice to meet you—"

"Wait," Dusty said, scrambling to retrieve money from her backpack, "I owe you."

"No, you don't. My treat this time."

Before Dusty could argue, Ali had flashed a parting smile and turned into a line of people headed out of the room.

Dusty watched her, every long, smooth step, every turn of her head until she was out of sight. No one had ever captured her attention so completely. She wanted to know more about Ali, everything about her. What did she think, what made her laugh, what made her cry? Everything. Yes, she wanted to know everything.

Dusty shouldered her backpack, returned the tray, and followed two sorority sisters through the heavy wooden door before she realized—she hadn't addressed the usual question, the one that should have crowded to the top right away. Was she gay? Only now the question emerged from the cloud that was Ali Nichols. A beautiful, mesmerizing cloud. So, was she? Had there been a sign hidden in the cloud? The search for it had already begun, the replaying of every moment, every fascinating moment. It was a search Dusty welcomed.

Chapter Six

Today was girls' day out. Saturday this week; some weeks it was Sunday. It was Jada's time with her mother, and her father's way of making sure that his wife had time away for girl things.

"I'm stealing your best girl for the day, Papa," Jada said, entering her childhood home.

He was in the front room, standing in front of the TV with the remote. "You gonna leave me alone to watch the Tigers' closer lose another one for them?"

"We are indeed," she replied with a laugh.

He returned the laugh. "Well, it's a torture I wouldn't wish on either of you. If it weren't for my weird hope that *this* time they'd pull it out, I'd be mowing the yard."

"Good enough excuse, I'd say." The whir of her mother's electric wheelchair captured their attention. "Hey, are you ready?" Jada asked.

"Just grab my purse off the table there, will you?"

Jada retrieved the purse and smiled. As usual her mother had taken the time to fix her hair as attractively as possible despite the fact that they were headed to the hairdresser's first. Mitch Baker leaned down and kissed his wife. "All right," he said, "Jada, don't forget to leave me your car keys. I set aside enough for bail money in case I have to come and get you. And don't tell me what you have planned so I can honestly say that I don't know anything about it." He kissed Jada on the cheek. "Thank you, honey."

Gracie Baker easily navigated the metal ramp and the van lift and settled into the specially equipped van. There wasn't anything that her husband hadn't done to make life easier for her. Doorways had been widened, kitchen and bathroom counters lowered, and upper cabinets equipped with pull-down shelves. Reminders every time Jada was there of just how much her father loved her mother.

In many ways there was an unusual mother/daughter bond—one that skipped a good amount of teenage angst and rebellion. Coming out early at fourteen and having a mother who didn't panic surely shaped their course. "I thought it could be a phase," she'd said later, "a part of growing up. I had had my crushes, too."

But when it wasn't and a crush at sixteen graduated from dreams and overnight soul talks to kisses and awakened desire, Gracie Baker did what many parents do not. She asked questions, she read, and she listened. And she talked to her husband—long enough and calmly enough so that he, too, listened.

It wasn't as if the usual fears weren't there, they were: Could her daughter find the happiness and commitment that she had? Would she be safe and free of destructive condemnation? Would she ever be totally accepted by a still evolving society? And it wasn't as if her fears weren't legitimate; they truly were. But Gracie never tried to change her daughter; she tried to understand who she was. She joined the local chapter of PFLAG and shared knowledge and experiences with other parents, and became her daughter's strongest advocate. Jada was well aware that she was blessed with a mother that young lesbians longed for, and almost losing her had cemented their bond.

▽　▽　▽

Carla always positioned Gracie's wheelchair next to the chair of Jada's hairdresser, Jeri. Sharing the conversation added a good dose of humor to the day. Gracie called it "salon standup." And they both loved it.

Carla ran her fingers through Gracie's hair, checked its length and said, "Okay, gorgeous, what are we doing today? Has Jada convinced you to let me have my way with your hair yet?"

"Come on, Mom," Jada added, "try something different. Let's surprise Dad."

Gracie watched Carla in the mirror. "I don't want to give the poor man a heart attack."

"Oh, trust me," Carla replied, "a beautiful, young-looking wife isn't going to give him a heart attack."

Jeri snickered and Jada grinned at her mother in the mirror. The scale tipped.

"What would you do?" Gracie asked with a hint of mischief in her eyes.

"I'd go shorter, get the bulk of this off your neck," Carla said, eyeing her customer's reaction in the mirror. "And add some color."

Gracie looked immediately to Jada as Jeri's clippers hummed a cleanup of Jada's neckline. "How short?" she asked.

"Don't panic," Carla replied. "We won't go that short."

"Trust her," Jada said. "She knows what she's doing."

"Well, with hair at least," Jeri added with a raspy laugh.

"Okay," Gracie relented. "Just remember you're not working on a millennial."

"So you're saying that I can't use that awesome pink I was planning on?"

"Now you're just trying to scare me," Gracie replied.

"All right, I'm not telling you anything else."

"Okay," Gracie said. "I'm closing my eyes and taking my chances."

Carla grinned. "Good girl. We're going to knock his argyles into next week."

"Oh my God." Another raspy laugh from Jeri. "Then we need to figure out something that'll knock Geoff's socks off *before* he gets in the house. The only good those things can offer is fumigating the house. Even insects and vermin steer clear."

"Well, hell then," Carla said, "have a pair of those walk themselves over to my house. I was in the basement doin' laundry yesterday and the biggest spider I've ever seen greeted me in the laundry tub. He was all black and hairy, smokin' a cigarette and had an 'I Love Mom' tattoo on one arm. I don't even remember how I got back up those stairs—maybe backward. Shit. I'm just gonna go *buy* new underwear."

You could tell by Gracie's eyes, laughter wetting their corners, how much she enjoyed the monthly stories, the humor found in the ridiculous. Jada was sure that if Gracie had her druthers the stand-up team would be doing her hair for her funeral—no doubt still laughing at their antics. "So," Gracie managed, "I need to be grateful for Mitch's dry cracked feet and flip-flops."

"Hey," Jeri added, "you find those blessings, wherever they are, write those beauties on Post-it notes and put 'em where you can see them every day."

Carla couldn't resist. "I don't think the Post-its are going to drown out the sound of mini Harleys from the spider gang in the basement."

There was just enough of a cool breeze to favor the outdoor café that her mother loved. Less noise, easy wheelchair access, and food that even Gracie couldn't match at home. "A bit of a splurge," she always said. "Just because we can."

They were enjoying the last of their lunch, and Jada ordered Arnold Palmer refills. While she admired her mother's new 'do—medium brown undertones and wide streaks of blond swept back over one ear—Gracie looked up. "What?" she asked, returning her daughter's smile.

"I really like your hair like that. Are you glad you did it?"

"We still got served," she replied with a shrug. "And I didn't send the kids at the next table running, so I'm hoping that it looks as good as I feel."

"Oh, good," Jada said, relaxing against the back of her chair. "I was worried that we all talked you into something you would regret."

"I've never been easily talked into anything. Just ask your father."

"Speaking of," Jada said, "do you think he will like it?"

"As long as I like it, he'll like it. I never worry about that," she said. "I didn't do it to please him. I did it for me— because I like how it makes me feel to do something fresh and different."

"Like you are put together as well on the outside as you are on the inside—or the feeling you get from clean sheets, or the first deep breath of fresh spring air."

Gracie nodded. "Right. That's how I feel." She tilted her head and smiled at her daughter. "We're a lot alike, aren't we?"

In what made most people feel good, sure. And beyond that, in their compassion, in their loyalty to family and friends, and, of course, in their cravings for ice cream and chocolate. "We are," Jada agreed. And then in the next moment doubted that her mother in any way could identify with her devious teenage daughter sneaking off to claim promised kisses behind the bleachers from the captain of the cheerleading squad. Or the lies, those initial cover stories that her good friend Daniel was her boyfriend and that much of the time that she was supposed to be some-where with him, she was skin to skin in Annie's bedroom while *her* mother was working. No. Jada was 99.9 percent, bet-the-farm, sure-as-a-Catholic-pope that Gracie had never done *that*.

It did make her wonder, though, what secrets of her mother's early years might be tucked away in parental propriety. There had been at least one serious boyfriend before her father. Gracie cherished the beautiful cherry china cabinet that he had handmade for her. Had he had a parental stamp of approval? Or had she needed to sneak out to see him? What happened to break them up? Had it been meeting her father, home on leave at the church picnic? Jada had heard the story, more than once. From her mother who described the handsome young soldier who neatly folded his jacket and organized the football game, making sure that both boys and girls were included on each team. From her father who claimed that he ate five pieces of pie because the prettiest girl there was manning the dessert table. And from her Aunt Katherine, who swore that she thought the sparks between them would surely start the August grass on fire.

The rest she had learned on her own, from sneaking into her mother's closet and reading his letters to her, stored in a shopping bag in the corner. They told her more about her father than she could have gleaned anywhere else. The letters were filled with longing in sensitive, heart-felt prose—longing for home, longing for time to hold her and dream of a life together. And there were sweet, romantic poems, along with daily records of life in a war zone. But Jada's favorite letter—one that she read over and over again—was where he asked his Gracie if he made it home after that deployment, would she take his hand and never let go. Each time she read it she saw a brave young soldier sitting on the edge of a cot asking the woman he loved to marry him. It brought tears every time, and planted a hope for her own life. A hope that as she matured had taken on a cloud of doubt.

Gracie scooped the last of her nearly melted ice cream and topped the last bite of chocolate brownie. "Oh, honey, what's wrong?" she said, noticing Jada's half-eaten dessert. "You always finish before I do."

"Oh," Jada replied, "no, I was thinking, that's all."

"Must be pretty important if it takes your attention away from chocolate."

Her look was contemplative. "What was it about Dad that made him the one?"

"Hmm." Gracie's expression brightened beyond her favorite dessert. "At first, it was how his eyes danced—even when there didn't seem to be a reason."

"They still do."

"Uh, huh. And all the time I was enjoying the dance, he was showing me every day how much he respected what I had to say, and that he loved to make me laugh." She smiled at her own revelation. "Then one day after he had been interviewing for jobs all day, he picked me up and took me to a movie that I so wanted to see. Fifteen minutes into the movie he fell asleep. That's when I realized it—he always put me first, from the first day I met him."

"You picked a good one, Mom."

"I did, didn't I?" She tilted her head and looked squarely at her daughter. "What about you, Jada? I want you to find someone and be happy."

"I want that, too," Jada replied. "Not that I'm *not* happy. I think I'm basically a happy person, but . . ."

"It's better to share your life with someone special."

"You and Dad have always been able to count on each other and trust each other, haven't you? Even when things were tough."

"Especially when things were tough. I always knew we would be okay." Gracie reached over and covered Jada's hand. "There are ways that you know, things that seem so small but mean so much. I don't know if he'd even remember it, but we had to go to this hoity-toity affair a couple of months after you were born. All these bigwigs were there—full course dinner and entertainment—way too fancy for my taste. But I never said anything, even though I hadn't lost the baby weight and I had to buy bigger shoes and a size sixteen dress. But he knew without me saying a word. He leaned over and whispered in my ear, 'You are the prettiest girl here.'"

"Aww, my dad the sweet-talker."

"And you know, it didn't matter that it wasn't true or if I believed it. What was important was that instinctively he knew to say it."

"So I'm looking for a loyal, romantic, intuitive woman to share my life with."

"Well, there may have to be a bit of chemistry mixed in there," Gracie said with a coy grin.

"Oh, yeah, that."

"So there you have it," Gracie said, as if the secret combination had been revealed. "Why did you stop seeing Marsha? She seemed really sweet."

"She is," Jada replied, "and smart and compassionate. But she loves teaching and she needs someone who can live in the closet with her—separate apartment, fake boyfriend, someone who won't jeopardize her career—and I'm not that person. I can't pretend to be someone I'm not, and I can't put her at risk."

"One of the PFLAG mothers has a daughter who teaches and she is out."

"But there's no protection, Mom. All it takes is a change in school administration and she could be fired. I know Marsha isn't willing to take that chance."

"Don't give up, honey," Gracie said, patting her daughter's hand. "She's out there, somewhere."

Jada smiled at her mother's encouragement. "I'm not sure that what you and Dad have is possible for me. But we'll see. Meanwhile I'm preoccupied with an infatuation with the vet who's taking care of the kittens."

"Infatuation?"

"Mmm, huh. I'm letting myself get lost in caramel-colored eyes and the sound of her voice."

"And chemistry?"

"TMI, Mom," Jada replied with a smile. "Besides, chemistry takes two. This is just infatuation—something that makes me smile before I go to sleep at night."

Chapter Seven

Lansing, Michigan, 2017

"... And remember Poland where last month the government passed an anti-abortion law and six million women turned out in the streets and they had to change it. We are the people. We have people power and we will use it.... This is an outpouring of energy and true democracy like I have never seen in my very long life. It is wide in age. It is deep in diversity. And remember the Constitution does not begin with 'I, the president.' It begins with 'We the people.'"

Gloria Steinem, The Women's March, Washington, DC, January 21, 2017

The signs ran the gamut; the resistance covered so many fronts. "1968 is Calling—Don't Answer," "Power To The Pussy," "I Am German, I've Seen This Before," "90 years A Nasty Woman," "The ACA Saved My Life."

Thousands of signs, homemade, heart-made, by thousands of women and men uniting in resistance. The streets of Lansing were packed, shoulder to shoulder, with ten thousand plus, by an early count.

Jada couldn't describe what it was that she was feeling,

but she loved it. She loved being part of the slow-moving mass as it filled the veins of the capital. There was a power to it, to so many people uniting and speaking as one. Knowing that what she believed was being held up and demanded by all those people surrounding her was the most powerful thing she had ever felt. She stepped with determination and chanted confidently. It was exhilarating. A high that lifted her above the fog that had fallen over everything. And she was sharing it with a woman who was becoming more important to her by the day.

Amie hooked her arm with Jada's and chanted with her. "This is what democracy looks like!" Each time the woman with the bullhorn asked, "What does democracy look like?" the throng answered. And each time Jada said the words, the more she believed them, the more she believed *in* them. In so many ways she did not want this day to end. She wanted to carry this feeling with her, to allow its power to overcome the stress of her workday, to ease the concerns that kept her awake at night.

For now, though, for today she was part of a bigger power, allowing the mass of energy and strength to carry her hope for things to get better.

All the way home she shared the energy and sense of inclusion with Amie and hospital staff Sharon and Mary. They all felt it, and all vowed to find ways to contribute, to do their part to resist, and to keep the feeling of hope that today had given them.

It was the best Jada had felt since the election, and her smile as Amie stopped the car in front of the house showed it. "I haven't seen *that* smile," Amie remarked. "Today was good, then."

"It was—it still is," Jada replied. "I don't want it to end." The nuance in the intimacy of her tone and the lingering of her gaze wasn't missed.

It was matched. "I don't either." Amie hesitated a moment, then added, "Should I stay and talk?"

"Yes, you should."

Amie pulled her car into the drive before Jada felt a watered-down version of her normal concern about the condition of her house. Today was weekly cleaning day and it hadn't got done—but for good reason.

"It's tiny," Jada said as they entered the little cottage, "but the rent is right and the utilities low." She grabbed up a pair of sweats draped over the back of the overstuffed chair and picked up the laundry basket from the couch that filled a large percentage of the space in the one room that served as a living and dining room. She disappeared through a doorway and reemerged to find Amie gazing at a picture of Jada's mother and father, occupying a small table next to the chair.

"Your parents?" Amie asked.

"Uh, huh. Just after my dad's last tour. She still says how blessed she feels that he came home with all his pieces."

"Proud in his uniform," Amie added with another look at the picture.

"He's a proud man—and very angry right now for more reasons than you or I can know."

"I can only imagine."

"One of my mother's special gifts is keeping my father grounded."

"You look like your mother." Amie turned her head, only a breath away from Jada's face. "She's beautiful."

Jada met the eyes, intent on her own, and they caught her breath short. She pulled her eyes away quickly and regretted it immediately. She hadn't felt that feeling in a long while—that moment like no other, filled with excitement and wonder, just before the first touch, the first paralyzing moment that happens only once. And she wanted that moment again—wanted it with Amie. But she had dismissed it, turned it down.

"We almost lost her five years ago," was Jada's best recovery. The space widened between them, but Jada's heartbeat kept its pace. "A bad car accident. She was crushed from the waist down."

"Oh, Jada, I'm so sorry."

"She's in a wheelchair and able to do a lot, but I was never as frightened as I was when I first saw her in the hospital. It was awful. I didn't want to leave her side for fear that I would never see her alive again." Tears were never far from that vision, that memory, and they collected now in her eyes.

Amie saw them, concern showing in the press of her brow. She took Jada's hand and held it in both of her own.

"My dad was lost; he just paced and paced. I didn't know how to help him. I searched for a way. All I could do was stay by my mom's side while he logged miles of hallway."

"He must know," Amie said. "*They* must know how much you love them."

Jada offered an acknowledging smile. "I hit the parental pool jackpot," she said, lightening her tone. "Mom doesn't let an opportunity go by to let me know how much she wants me to go back to school. It bothers her that I quit to take care of her."

"Do you want to go back?"

"Sometimes the dream outshines reality." She was comfortable in the caramel-colored gaze and aware that Amie hadn't let go of her hand. "I was so excited to be on my own, to learn and explore, to figure out what I wanted to do in my life." Jada turned toward the couch, slipped her hand away and pushed the pillows into the corner. They sat, Jada with her shoulder pressed against the back, and Amie relaxed into the pillows.

"Would you go back to school if you could?"

"I don't know," she replied with a shrug. "I didn't have time to narrow things down—maybe if I already had a focus. I have taken a couple of night classes, partly because it made my mom so happy, but . . . it's just that now I want my limited time and money to count, to apply to something that counts."

Amie was nodding as if she understood. Maybe she did. Maybe she wanted to. But Jada wondered how she could—someone like her, so focused and accomplished. "Did you always know what you wanted to do?"

"If you count playing doctor when I was five, I suppose." Amie smiled. "I've been lucky in so many ways. Second of four kids, dad's a pediatrician—I grew up imagining I was dad's helper. I 'took care' of everything smaller than me—kids, pets, wild animals. So I guess it was a natural progression."

"I think you *are* a natural. And I'm very glad you're taking care of my babies."

"Not for much longer. They're ready to come and challenge you to kitten-proof this place."

"Oh," Jada exclaimed with a quick look around. "Oh, I've got work to do."

"Just remember that there is virtually nowhere they can't get to. They need lots of distractions."

"Yes," Jada replied, "I remember. But it's been a while. I need to do some shopping."

"With two of them," Amie said as she stood, "maybe you should find room for a playscape."

Jada surveyed the limited space of the living/dining room. It would have to be here, somehow. The bedroom barely housed a full-sized bed and small dresser, and the kitchen—well, two steps by six was a nonstarter even if she ever considered encouraging felines to play in a kitchen. "Possibly if I move the computer desk to the corner, I could put the playscape in front of the window. That way they could watch what was going on outside."

"Hey, I have an idea," Amie began as she moved toward the door. "The lady who takes in animals, the one who has the rest of the kittens, makes playscapes for a little bit of nothing. I'll bet she could make one that would fit, plus you'd get to see the other kittens."

"I would love to—" she began just as Amie turned into the tight space between them.

"Tomorrow?" Amie asked on a soft breath that reached Jada's cheek. The gaze, the moment was about more than tomorrow.

And so was Jada's answer. "Yes," she said as Amie's hand slid around to the small of Jada's back. Paralyzed in the moment, Jada was held captive in Amie's gaze. She didn't move, didn't close the narrow gap, didn't take the moment. Instead she felt herself pulled into an embrace, the length of her body pressed into Amie's. Held there long enough to breathe in the subtle scent of her perfume, to feel the quickening beat of Amie's heart competing with her own. Long enough for the smooth, soft skin of Amie's cheek to slide against her own, for the words "sleep well" to be whispered against her ear. Then Amie claimed the moment Jada had thought was gone. She kissed her—gently enough to tease her intent, firmly enough to leave a spark, a warmth that would linger for hours.

Chapter Eight

It was all Jada could think of before she fell asleep, all she could dream of once she did. That kiss, claiming her thoughts and dreams, had taken them into an exciting, uncharted space. It was theirs to navigate now, theirs to define. The memory of it woke her early and excited her morning. She hustled through her tasks, her thoughts sparking with anticipation.

This time the house would be clean, the laundry done, and she'd even had time to measure for the playscape. She dried off from her shower, rubbed the towel through her hair, and grabbed the phone from the back of the toilet. No text from Amie yet, and fifteen minutes to get dressed.

"Okay," she mumbled, staring at the open dresser drawer, "what to wear, what to wear?" Cool enough today for jeans. V-neck pullover or blue-striped shirt? Peach looked better with her hair, so she smiled to herself and pulled out the V-neck. When was the last time it mattered this much? The company Christmas party? No, not *this* much. First date with the elementary teacher? Maybe. But right now, nothing felt more important than this time.

She hurriedly dressed and fastened small gold hoops to her ears next to the gold studs just as her phone signaled a text message. Amie was waiting at the light two blocks away. Jada scooped up her keys, locked the front door, and let her heart race to the end of the driveway.

As the silver Subaru approached, Jada struck a pose with one hand on her hip and the other thumb up for a ride.

Amie stopped the car and greeted Jada with a bright smile and, "I normally don't pick up hitchhikers, but I will not be responsible for leaving someone so cute on the street. You never know who might try to pick you up."

"Well, I'm very careful who I get in a car with." Well, there *was* the strange woman helping her look for Sweetness, but . . .

"Is that right?"

"Oh, yeah, I don't accept a ride from just anyone. They have to have a car that looks like they care, not new, just maintained. They have to be female, have a smile that makes me want to smile back, and honest eyes."

"So that's why you got in my car?"

Jada shook her head "no." "*Your* smile does much more than make me smile back—and your eyes may be saying more than you want them to."

"They're saying exactly what I want them to." Amie leaned across the console and slipped her hand around the back of Jada's neck.

Jada lowered her eyes and leaned forward to meet the soft, warm lips. She moved against the warmth—gently, sensuously—expecting the spark of heat slowly moving through her body, wanting it to lead where she knew it would.

Amie lifted her lips a slight tease away, and brushed tender touches over Jada's lips and cheeks. "You kept me awake last night," she whispered.

Jada tilted her head back with a smile. "Then I wasn't the only one."

"No, you weren't," she replied, holding Jada's gaze. "Is this where you saw us going?"

"Only in those secret wishes that rarely come true."

A car squeezed around the Subaru on the narrow street. "We should probably get going," Amie said, settling back into the driver's seat. She looked back at Jada with a tilt of her head. "It *was* up to me, wasn't it? To make the first move?"

"I wasn't sure that I was reading everything right. I didn't want to do something that would ruin even a friendship."

Amie smiled and shook her head. "After all those signals I sent. I invaded your personal space every chance I had."

"I know."

The drive, lined with mature maples, wound back from the main road for some distance before Jada could realize the size of the barn partly hidden behind the old farmhouse.

"Wow," Jada exclaimed, "when you said that she had lots of room you weren't exaggerating."

"She has twenty-five acres and a heart as big as her barn." Amie parked the car in front of the big barn doors. "Any animal that she can't find a home for stays right here with great care and a whole lotta love. Come on," she said, opening the car door. "She said she'll be in the barn."

A black lab with a muzzle more white than black greeted them at the corner of the building. "Jake checks out all visitors," Amie explained. "A bark is a warning, and his tail wagging like this means we check out." Amie scratched his head and neck, and Jake followed them to the side door of the barn. A curious pony lifted her head over the top of the wire fence attached to the back of the barn as the women opened the door.

"Dusty?" Amie called as they entered the large cement-floored structure. Big overhead fluorescents lighted the interior.

"Down here," Dusty called back, stepping into view from the far end of the barn.

As they started in her direction, a dog's face peered from behind Dusty's legs. A second later the dog was barreling toward the women at full speed.

"Sweetie! Oh, Sweetie!" Jada exclaimed just before one leap landed her flat on her back with Sweetie whining and covering her face with a large wet tongue. "Okay, okay," she managed between licks. "I know. Yes, I missed you, too."

"Come on, girl," Dusty said with a tug on Sweetie's harness. "Come on, you got to let her get up."

Whining and wiggling from head to tail, Sweetie backed up enough for Jada to get to her feet. She pulled against Dusty's hold to press her face against Jada's stomach. "Oh, my God, it's my sweet girl," Jada exclaimed. "I can't believe it!"

"Are you all right?" Amie asked. "You went down hard."

"No, I'm good, I'm good," she replied as Amie gently brushed the back of Jada's shirt.

"I'm sorry," Dusty added. "She was gone before I could grab her."

"Oh, yes, introductions," Amie said. "Dusty Logan, this is Jada Baker, and it looks like everyone knows Sweetie here."

"How did she get here?" Jada asked, as she knelt and wrapped her arms around the thick neck and kissed Sweetie's head. "I was sure I would never see my sweet girl again."

"People know that if they see an animal in trouble they can bring it here. They're safe here, and I do all I can to find them a loving home. But I'm telling you, this dog is such a joy," Dusty replied, "and the most loving dog, and unless you are able to give her a good home with you, she's here to stay. She rarely leaves my side, well, except," she motioned toward Jada and smiled. "She knows who saved her."

"They all seem to, don't they?" Amie added.

Dusty nodded. "And they repay with unconditional love

and loyalty. And speaking of saving, you're the one responsible for the kittens?"

"Oh, yes, thank you so much for taking them." She planted another kiss to Sweetie's head and stood. "How are they doing?"

"Well, we'll let the doc here tell us what she thinks. Momma tabby and the whole brood have their own condo." Dusty motioned for them to follow her.

They headed back toward the other end of the barn, past a wall of kennels, each with its own exit to the outside. Each kennel had stainless bowls and some version of a dog bed. "Most of the dogs are out in the play yard right now, except these two. I still have to see how social Buddy here is." The mixed terrier pushed his nose through the bars and Dusty stoked it gently. "And Cissy," as she moved to the next kennel where a ball of brown fur was curled in the bed, "sleeps a lot right now. She's recovering from heartworm treatment. By the way . . ." She directed the comment to Jada. "We got Sweetie in time to be treated. She had heartworms, too."

"Oh, wow, I didn't even think about that."

"It's one of the first things I check." Dusty stopped in front of an elevated wooden hutch. The interior was a blur of little fur babies, rolling and wrestling and playing on a cushy pad covering the bottom of the hutch. "They play as much as they sleep now, and momma's spending increasingly more time away from them."

"She's earned those breaks," Amie said, reaching in and picking up a little gray and white kitten. "If they all have tummies like this one, then she's done a fine job of fattening them up." She handed the kitten to Jada, picked up two more of the foster babies, and checked them over. "Eyes are all clear, no runny noses, and nice round bellies. So far, everything looks good. Have you started solid food?"

"Uh, huh, they're eating good. I feed them while momma's out. Next week they're due for second deworming."

Amie finished checking each of the babies and placed the last one back in the hutch. "Can you bring them in sometime next week for their vaccinations? And they will need a booster in a month."

"Sure," Dusty replied.

"I wish I could just come out and do it here, but corporate management won't allow it. A lot of things besides the new building changed when Blake's sold."

Dusty nodded. "The new office manager seems rather stiff. The girls at the desk have always been so personable, but when she is within earshot they don't even smile."

"The cohesiveness of the staff isn't the same with the new doctors that they brought in. None of them want to do on-call duty, and they frown on our silliness. We were more of a family before, sharing and respecting each other's professional opinions. I really miss that."

"I've gotten so that I ask for an appointment with you or one of the original vets," Dusty added, "who I know won't treat me like a number or a dollar sign. I know that the animals I bring you will get care from your hearts. I trust that."

"We'll try our best to always deserve that trust."

"My babies count on it." Dusty looked to Jada. "I'll show you around if you have time."

"I'd love that," she replied and turned to Amie. "Do we have time?"

"Sure. You need to see what this lady does."

It was admirable, Jada thought, the number of animals, the amount of work—and the cost. She couldn't even imagine how much food, health care, and merely maintaining this place must cost. It clearly took more than heart. She watched Dusty in the play yard with the dogs and in the cat compound and the pasture with two rescued horses and the curious pony, and one thing was apparent above all else: Dusty Logan was a compassionate and committed woman. And Jada liked her—a lot.

"You've got to meet Rudy," Dusty said as they neared the

pasture gate. She had the run of the yard around the house. "Sweetie," she directed, "go find Rudy. Where is she?"

Sweetie snapped to attention. Ears up, she looked toward the house, then raced off, disappearing around the corner. "In the animal world, Rudy is her best friend. She absolutely loves her."

"Oh, Rudy," Amie said. "I did the surgery on her leg."

"One of her front legs was so deformed that she couldn't walk on it," Dusty explained. "The good doctor here gave her a quality of life that even I didn't think possible."

"Surgery can only do so much," Amie said with a nod to Dusty. "Without your commitment to her therapy, she would never be running like *that*." She drew their attention to a little floppy-eared brown and white goat hopping and running alongside a happy Sweetie.

"Oh, Dusty," exclaimed Jada, "how cute is that?"

Sweetie alternated excited kisses to Rudy's head and to Jada as she knelt beside them. The little goat stopped hopping and nuzzled her head against Sweetie's neck.

The women petted and fussed over the pair until the sound of a vehicle approaching on the gravel drive captured their attention.

"Ah," Dusty began, "Rory's here with supplies."

The shiny red Ford truck pulled to a stop next to the big barn door, and Rory jumped from the cab with a smile. "I see you've met our very own animal kingdom anomaly," he said. "If we're smart, we'll use their bestie footage on the website. Right, Doc?"

"Hey, Rory," Amie greeted. "I would say absolutely. Good trust factor for people to board here, and an excellent tug at the heart for donations for the rescues. Yep," she said, with a rub to their heads as she stood, "they're perfect."

"I'm sure they are," Dusty replied, "but that website is in dire need of updating, and unless Rory here is willing to tackle it, it just isn't happening. This ol' girl is a tech moron and not afraid to admit it."

"I'll see if I can figure it out," replied Rory. "If not, I'll put the word out that we need charity or a cheap rate. Maybe we'll be lucky enough to find another Jerry. I miss that guy in so many ways."

"I could do it for you," Jada offered. "It's the least I can do, for taking care of Sweetie and the kittens."

"Oh, for God's sake," Dusty interjected. "I didn't even introduce you. I guess manners are the first to go. I'm sorry," she said, motioning to Jada. "Rory Jackson, this is Jada Baker."

"It's a pleasure," he said, offering his fist for a fist bump.

Dusty's expression was an unconvincing scowl. "You didn't just fist bump her."

Rory turned his head over a jutted shoulder. "I, for one, don't feel the need to act my age."

"Of course you don't," Dusty said with a smile.

"Just one more reason you love me," he added, backing toward the truck. "I'll get the feeding started."

"We should get going," Amie said. "I have a menagerie of sorts of my own—all hungry and some crossing their legs by now."

"Okay," Jada replied. "But I am serious about the website." She looked from Rory to Dusty. "Who will I be working with?"

Dusty shook her head. "Tech moron, remember? You're working with Mr. Handsome there; that is, if I can afford you."

"No, really, it's my way of paying you back for taking care of Sweetie and the kittens."

"No need. Would've done it anyway. You tell me what your time is worth and I'll pay you."

"Don't argue with her," Rory said. "It's a sweet deal."

Dusty raised her hands in submission. "All right."

Jada smiled. "Next Saturday then?" She directed to Rory.

"Next Saturday it is," he replied.

64

Dusty stood next to Rory at the back of the truck and watched as Amie's car made its way down the drive.

"So," Rory began, "did I just meet one of those millennials that you swear think our generation is shrouded in dinosaur dust? The one who just offered to do our website without any obvious condescension?"

"You don't know what she's thinking."

"Well, we'll see. I do know one thing for sure, though. She makes even this old queen look twice."

"Well, I'm right about something, too. Dr. Amie is in love with her."

"You think so, seriously? Is it mutual?"

"Not sure she knows it, but yeah. You should have seen them before you got here. Private looks, adoring smiles, casual touches. I swear sometimes you couldn't get a piece of paper between them."

"Well, now you're making my toes tingle," he said with a grin. "And it makes me happy for Doc. I was afraid she had stopped looking."

"Maybe she wasn't looking," Dusty said, pulling a large bag of cat food from the truck. "That seems to be when good things happen."

"She's one of a kind," Amie remarked as the farm disappeared from the rearview mirror. "I've never met anyone like her."

Jada nodded. "Her commitment is remarkable. How does she do it all?"

"She boards animals to fund some of it, and donations help. Thank you, by the way, for offering help with the website. That's the main source of donations."

"It makes me wonder what she must sacrifice in order to take on such a commitment. Even with Rory it has to be a full-time job."

Amie glanced quickly at Jada. "You know, I wonder that,

65

too. And to say that I've known her for three years isn't true because I don't really *know* her. She offers nothing beyond the care of those animals, and I haven't asked."

"Have you wanted to?"

"Many times. I've just never felt comfortable enough."

"Do you think she's a lesbian?"

Another quick glance. "She *should* be." Amie added a smile. "But confident, accomplished, single straight women have fooled me before. So I wouldn't bet a paycheck on it."

"What about Rory?"

"He's gay. A number of his friends bring their pets in to me. They know I am, and chitchat with them has made it obvious that he is. But no one has ever said anything about Dusty, and nobody I know has seen her at any LGBT events."

"So, does Dusty know about you?"

"Probably. I've been out to my family since I was eighteen, and out at work since the first coworker asked me out. It's not something I hide."

"So, is she straight," Jada asked, "or stuck in the dark ages?"

Amie offered a quiet laugh.

"You know, they set up house in a closet and are now too afraid to step out of it."

"If she is, it must be a lonely existence, then *and* now. I'd be very uncomfortable if I couldn't be myself with my family or straight friends."

Jada nodded. "I wouldn't consider them friends if they didn't even know who I was. And if they didn't like who I was, I wouldn't want them in my life. Being who you are cuts through a lot of wasted time, it seems."

"True," Amie agreed, turning onto Jada's street. "With all this curiosity, and a lot of it having nothing to do with her sexuality, maybe we ought to get to know Dusty Logan a little better."

"I'm in," Jada answered with a smile. "You know, it's possible that Dusty thinks younger people aren't interested in her life."

Amie brought the car to a stop in front of the house. "There are a lot of things that I'm interested in."

"Oh?" Jada leaned across the console and slid her hand over the flat plane below Amie's chest. "Like what?"

"Do you need me to tell you?"

"Yes," Jada said softly, "I do."

Amie leaned forward and whispered the words, "I'm interested in everything about you." She touched her lips to Jada's cheek. "Everything." Then tenderly to her lips. "What makes you happy. What you want."

Jada closed the distance of a whisper and pressed firmly into a kiss—open and warm. "This," she breathed before a kiss that deepened into exploration shot sensations to her core, and promised so much more.

Chapter Nine

1971

A series of bare bulbs hanging from the rafters did their best to light the basement meeting room. Over the past months the array of mismatched chairs and their regular occupants had served as a grounding for Dusty, a place where her thoughts and opinions, otherwise afforded the importance of an unmatched sock, found solidarity and respect. Here she listened and was listened to. Here, with this potpourri of women, she realized the full scope of the inequity they faced. The discussions covered things like birth control, abortion, education, careers—taboo topics in much of these women's daily lives. Many of them had little or no support for their beliefs from friends or family, and none of them counted on the support of strangers.

We're feminists, they declared, willing to suffer the wrath of those who would keep women quiet, who would keep women locked in traditional roles. They were counting on each other and on the women like them across the country. And Dusty was happy to be counted among them—happy, energized, and infatuated.

From the beginning she had been drawn to the cause and its purpose, and had attached her personal goals to it.

But more apparently she was drawn to the woman who carried the torch. Like a moth to a bright light, Dusty found every opportunity to stay close to Ali Nichols. And Ali made it easy. There were petitions and flyers and signs to be made, meetings and rallies, and radio and newspaper interviews to prepare for. So much to be done, so much to help with. It was a mission—their mission. And according to Ali, Dusty made it fun. They shared stories and laughed and finished each project even after the others had left for home. And tonight was no exception.

The last of the regular group left the basement of the bookstore with a promise to be back tomorrow, leaving the two women alone. Ali began gathering partially finished signs, and directed her comments to Dusty. "Can you collect the boxes of markers? Katie's closing the store early tonight. So, if we want to get a couple of more signs done for tomorrow, we'll have to make them at my place."

"Okay. Do we need to take any other materials with us?"

"No, I've got enough there. Let's pick up something to eat on the way."

She'd been at Ali's apartment many times, picking up or dropping off projects and materials, and grabbing a bite to eat before rallies. Tonight, though, felt different. The pace was slower, less hurried. They picked up pizza and sodas, and laughed about having to eat on the counter to keep tomato sauce away from the signs spread out on the table.

"You know," Ali began, adding a piece of crust to the others on her plate, "this says something about us."

"What, eating pizza this late like we were college kids?"

"No, but that is a thought." Ali smiled. "I was thinking about how we started working on the signs first while the pizza sat on the counter getting cold."

"Does that make us obsessed?"

"Oh," Ali said, adding the subtle smile that seemed so personal to Dusty, "I prefer *passionate*. We're passionate women, Dusty."

"And committed."

"And strong."

"You want the last word, don't you?" Dusty asked.

"No," Ali replied with a raise of her eyebrows, "I want this conversation to continue."

"Okay," Dusty said, following Ali into the living room. "Do you consider us feminists?"

"Of course."

"Even with everything people are attaching to the word?"

"Claiming the word doesn't make them all true," Ali replied.

"And if some of them *are* true?"

They stood there in front of the sofa, neither of them making a move to sit down. Dusty couldn't turn away from the eyes that had captured her months ago. They stayed on her—wondering, analyzing, she wasn't sure. She was only sure of what they did to her, every time. They pulled her in, sent their electricity through her, and held her for as long as they wished. They moved over Dusty's face as she spoke.

"Then we own them," she said, "the best way we can." Ali turned toward the built-in shelves at the end of the room, leaving her words to sizzle in possibility.

It was a dance of words—a step here, a sway there—they both recognized, and both knew what it could mean.

"Do you have a choice of music?" Ali asked, motioning to a shelf of square tape boxes.

"Your apartment," Dusty replied, "your choice."

"Then you'll get my favorite."

Curious, Dusty moved to Ali's side to watch her load a tape onto a reel-to-reel machine.

"The purest sound," Ali explained, "and the only way to

do justice to this woman's voice. Are you familiar with Edith Piaf?"

"No," Dusty replied, "I'm a sheltered Motown girl."

"Then let me introduce you." Ali pulled a book from one of the shelves and handed it to Dusty.

"La Mo—"

"La Môme Piaf," Ali finished, "the Little Sparrow. A tiny woman with a powerful voice. She sings about the pull of love, the sensitivity and pain of it, with a voice that's raw in its honesty. I listen to her a lot. She feeds my soul."

Ali started the tape as Dusty examined the book. Pure, yes, the sound from the tape was pure, clean, absent the hiss that she hadn't really noticed before from records. Dusty read from the back jacket. "Piaf's songwriting and famous voice bore testimony to a life filled with love and loss, struggle and pain. Her brilliant career survived physical pain, addiction, and a world war." So what was it about this woman's life that spoke so personally to Ali? And her voice, yes, there was no question that it had a pull of its own—an earthy resonance that spoke beyond the lyrics—lyrics Dusty didn't understand.

What she did understand was how close Ali was, touching her now, her chest against Dusty's shoulder and sending her heart racing ahead of the music. She remembered reading a paragraph at the beginning of the book, but not what it said. Dusty turned her head to look only inches away into the eyes that were claiming her. "What song is this?"

"La Vie en rose," Ali answered softly, "Life in Pink."

The heat of their bodies, of the hand circling her waist radiated through her. How long had she imagined this, wished it, with Ali—and now leaving the wish behind in her dreams?

Ali leaned down and whispered the words. *"Des yeux qui font baisser les miens.* Eyes that gaze into mine."

Dusty held her eyes, let the music and the words speak for both of them.

"Un rire qui se perd sur sa bouche. A smile that is lost on his lips—"

Dusty turned into an embrace, into a kiss that made everything real. Long arms wrapped around her, held her firmly, as their kiss deepened. It was no dream, no imagination; it was the intimacy of their lips, new and now, starting something they both wanted, had both waited for.

Their lips parted slightly, enough for Dusty to whisper, "When did you know?"

Ali kissed her again, then smiled against her lips. She lifted her head to say, "That first day. The moment your eyes didn't match your words."

Dusty drew her lips along the muscle of Ali's neck and stopped to whisper next to her ear. "What took you so long?"

Ali tilted her head back with a smile. "I wanted one night, one night with no meetings, or newsletters, or people—just you."

Dusty answered with a trail of kisses down to the tender place at the base of Ali's neck. "Will tonight do?"

Words were no longer necessary. They both knew where they were headed, what they needed from each other. Their haven, the room backlit by the light from the kitchen, and a deep cushion couch was judged only by the privacy it provided. It was their private space and time filled with the sensuous sound of *La Môme Piaf.* Dusty wasn't aware that she was breathing, yet she was—or of thinking, which she was not. She was lost, wonderfully lost in sky blue and unwilling to find her way.

There was nothing else she wanted, nothing she needed—only the feeling of Ali's skin against her own, the wonderful hands finding her, defining her, sending sensations over her body. She breathed in the smell of her, the familiar perfume that took her back to that first day. It enveloped her, wrapped her in a mist that was distinctly Ali.

Dusty floated on the sound of the music, moved with the sensations taking over her body. The words were whispers over her neck and breasts. "You're beautiful." And were answered with quickened breaths.

"I've wanted this for so long," Dusty said, pressing into the rhythm of their bodies. Her hands explored the length of the long, smooth muscles of Ali's back and the round, firm muscles of her buttocks. She loved the feel of her, the smell of her, the taste of her, and more. She whispered, "I love you."

"Yes," Ali returned between deepening kisses. "I want you, all of you."

It was right to let go, to give rein to the desire they both felt. They explored with hands and lips and found all the pleasurable places. Desire had its way, quickening their breaths and sending their heartbeats racing in anticipation. Tension wrapped them tightly, moving them with one purpose, one goal, their need for each other surging beyond control. Each kiss, deeper and more demanding, each stroke driving them closer and closer until the tension burst into orgasm. Dusty clung to Ali, breathing heavily against her as sensations continued in ripples of pleasure. She laid a trail of kisses along Ali's neck and across her shoulder.

Ali raised her head and kissed Dusty's face and lips, then held the gaze from her eyes. *Des yeux qui font baisser les miens,* she said softly.

"My eyes?" Dusty asked.

"Yes."

"What are they saying?"

"That I made you happy."

Dusty kissed her, moving gently against the soft lips, then whispered, "That you *make* me happy."

Chapter Ten

Jada took the last of the packages off the belt and stacked them in her truck. She was holding her tongue, holding her anger at the additional stops added to her already heavy route when Jerry tapped the box as he passed by.

"Watch yourself with that one," he said. "He's one scary dude."

"What?" she clipped, trying to remain civil. He was, after all, the reason for *that* one and the other added stops.

"If he's not there," Jerry said, closing the back door of his truck, "let the kid sign." Then he added, "Trust me."

Really? Jada thought. Trust me, from the guy whose route had just become much lighter at her expense.

Jada, as was her natural inclination, struggled through the morning to meet her deadlines. Struggling meant speeding on rural roads, skipping a break, and running each package to the door. Always looming in her subconscious was the threat of firing if stop numbers were not consistently met.

She checked the time, 9:56, and pulled into a neighborhood where she had been warned to watch her speed. Pushing the edge of the limit, Jada anxiously pulled the truck around the corner and down the street to the delivery address. She stopped, grabbed the package, jumped from the truck, and sprinted to the door. With four seconds to spare Jada rang the doorbell, and entered the delivery into the tracker.

Back in the truck, she climbed into her seat and dropped her head against the headrest. She had met the ten o'clock deadline, a relief more than physical. Once again she had met a big part of the company's commitment for the day. Then it occurred to her—Jerry had not been fired. He had consistently not met commitments, made it clear when others complained of impossible expectations that he would not speed, or give up breaks, or run packages to the door, and he had not been fired. Consciously or not, he was their test monkey.

Her posture relaxed against the back of the seat as she pulled into traffic and headed toward her next stop. Her hands loosened their grip on the steering wheel. With anger and anxiety pushed from her mind it was now clear that this was essentially a new route, and new numbers would have to be established. And whatever she did today would establish the base for those new numbers. So maybe it was Jerry in her ear, or just common sense taking over, but for the first time in a long time Jada drove the exact speed limit, took both breaks, and ate a lunch. She walked each delivery to the door and took time for attention to each of her favorite dogs. At least the starting numbers were going to be realistic. It had been the least stressful workday she could remember—until the last stop.

The house, a simple single-story structure, sat two car lengths off a main rural road. Despite a non-running truck at the back of the drive, the little front yard was mowed neatly and showed vestiges of a woman's touch in the perennials flowering along the front of the porch. Jada retrieved a medium-sized box from the now empty truck and wondered how often she would be delivering to the "scary dude." She locked the truck door and crossed the dirt driveway toward the house. Before she reached the corner of the low unrailed porch, movement at the side of the house caught her attention. Lifted only slightly off the ground and peering from behind the tailgate of a truck leaning against the house was the head of a midsize dog.

Large, soulful eyes stayed on her as Jada set the package on the ground and knelt to get a better look. Light from the opposite end of the makeshift lean-to showed the dog lying on its side. Her ribs were prominent, and the slightly enlarged nipples were evidence of a recent litter.

"Hey, girl," she said softly. "How you doing, girl? Where are your babies?"

A voice startled her with the answer. "Aw, they all died."

Jada turned so quickly that she almost lost her balance. A boy she guessed to be about thirteen or fourteen stood directly behind her.

"Oh," Jada replied as she got to her feet. "I'm sorry. When did she have them?"

"Last week sometime," he said. "There was four of them."

Another look at the dog and it was clear to Jada that there hadn't been enough milk to feed even one puppy. And there was no doubt that she was starving. Jerry's warning set the parameter for what she said next.

"Is your mother or father home?" She picked up the package. "I'll need a signature for this."

"Naw. When he ain't here, I sign it."

"Okay, sure."

He used his finger and signed his name on the electronic screen. *Ricky Jenkins.*

"Thanks, Ricky," she said, handing him the box. "Hey, would it be okay if I give your dog a treat? I always like to give the dogs on my route something. That way they aren't afraid of the truck."

He showed no expression in his hesitation to answer. For a moment, Jada wondered if he would answer at all. Then, "Yeah, I guess so."

"Oh, and while I'm getting treats, could you get her a bowl of water?"

"Eh, it'll just get tipped over."

"I'll hold onto it," Jada replied, trying to bridle her rising anger. "She'll be thirsty after the treats."

Another blank hesitation. "Yeah," he began hesitantly, "I guess it'll be okay."

Yeah, really? How long had it been since she'd had water, *clean* water? And when did she eat last? Anger was quickly shoving sadness aside. What kind of stupid allowed this? Or was it just outright meanness? Did it matter at this point, when the dog's best hope might be this less than reliable kid?

"The one day I eat all of my lunch," Jada muttered as she grabbed a handful of treats. When she returned, Ricky had brought out a bowl of water and, seeing it coming, the dog rose up enough to be able to drink. To his credit, Ricky held the bowl as she gratefully lapped the water.

"What's her name?" Jada asked.

"Mom called her Brandy, cause her color is like brandy wine. But she ain't here anymore."

"Well, that's still her name, don't you think?"

Ricky nodded.

"So was your mom the one who fed her and made sure that she had water?"

Another nod.

Jada offered one treat at a time, each barely crushed before being swallowed. "Maybe *you* could do that now."

He stood there with the empty bowl and that same blank hesitation.

"What do you think?" Jada prompted.

Finally, "I sneak her scraps when I clean up the dishes," he said. "But there ain't any dog food. Dad says it's her dog; he ain't payin' for it."

"What if I bring you a bag? Would you feed her every day?"

"It'll just make him mad."

She was starting to get a picture of the situation. This would be a decision she'd have to make later. New numbers on her route still had to be justified, and she'd already stretched this stop too long. "I know you're a good boy, Ricky. Maybe you can talk your dad into feeding her more—when he's in a really good mood."

Ricky didn't answer.

Jada headed back toward the truck, but turned to add encouragement. "Do your best, Ricky. She's counting on you."

Jada thought about it all the way back to the station. She could anonymously drop off a bag of food, put it on the porch when Ricky was at school or late at night. Who would turn down free food? Then again, after hours on the porch, it could end up being free food for the raccoons and squirrels. So, what if she just handed it to Ricky or his dad?

She caught sight of Jerry in the parking lot, getting his attention before he reached his car. "Hey, Jerry, can I ask your advice on something?"

"You can *ask*," he replied, but his smile told her that, as with most people, especially men, he was pleased at being asked.

"Did you see the dog at the Jenkins' house?"

"The scary dude? Yeah, poor scrawny thing."

"I think she's in really bad shape—like, starving." Jerry nodded. "I talked to the kid because his dad wasn't there."

"First-day luck," he said with a grin.

"Well, the kid told me that all she gets is scraps he sneaks out to her. His dad won't buy dog food because the dog was his wife's."

"Yeah, I guess that divorce was uglier than most. Neigh-

79

bors across the road saw a lot. When they hadn't seen her for a week, they thought he'd killed her."

"Whoa," she exclaimed. "No wonder the kid hesitated on every answer."

"I think the one thing that kid has going for him is a healthy fear of his father."

Healthy, an interesting description of fear. But she could see his point. Ricky was obviously concerned about making his father mad. "I hope I didn't convince him to do something, you know, to cross a line that he knows he shouldn't."

"Like what?"

"I asked him to see if it was okay for me to bring him a bag of dog food. I said that the dog is depending on him."

"Hopefully the kid knows better. It would piss his ol' man off."

"What if the food showed up on the porch anonymously?"

"What if the kid had already mentioned it to his dad?"

Jada frowned at the thought that she had already sabotaged that idea. "Why are you so sure that it's not worth trying?"

"I had an adult signature delivery for him and he wasn't there. I left a tag with the kid explaining that the signature had to be someone who is twenty-one or older, and I said that I'd reattempt the next day. So, the next day his ol' man met me in the middle of the driveway holding an AR-15 across his chest."

"Oh, shit!"

"*Yeah.* I did *not* want to get out of the truck. You know that ol' fight or flight thing had me shifting into reverse before he yelled, 'You got something for me?' It suddenly occurred to me that I was more apt to get shot if I tried to leave. So . . ." he shrugged.

"You delivered like a good soldier."

"And lived to ride again—after a barrage of obscenities and threats, and my promise that it wouldn't happen again."

"Thus, your warning to let the kid sign."

"I feel bad that you inherited that stop."

Jada offered a doubtful frown.

"No, I really do. You're all upset about the dog and all, and I don't think there's anything you can do about it."

"I can call the Humane Society."

"Don't give them your name or make a formal complaint."

"Seriously?"

"The neighbor said Jenkins is militia. I don't see any good reason to doubt it. Like I said"—Jerry retrieved the keys from his pocket and continued toward his car—"watch yourself."

It didn't take a lot of thought. Jada was compassionate, not self-destructive. She called the Humane Society as soon as she got home. They wanted all the expected information—address, condition of animal, availability of shelter, food, water—and she gave it in detail. They had just gotten to the personal information when Jada excused herself to answer the door.

The sight when she opened it brought the widest smile and the best feeling she had had all day. Amie, pet carrier and precious cargo in tow, returned the smile.

Jada motioned her in. "Just have to finish this call . . . yes, I'm back," she said into the phone. "What information do you need to send an investigator out?" Amie slipped past her with a kiss to her cheek. "So, it's not required . . . then no, I can't give that to you . . . yes I'm sure. Okay, thank you."

"Is everything okay?" Amie asked.

"Yes and no. I called the Humane Society to investigate the treatment of a dog on my route. She's in really bad shape. They need to step in and take her or she won't make it."

"Well, you did the right thing. That's part of their mission. They'll take care of it."

"I hope so."

Amie knelt beside the carrier. "Shall I let them out?"

"Oh, yes," she said, and watched as the kittens poked their heads hesitantly from their lair. "Welcome home, little ones."

They were typically curious, and it wasn't long before they were investigating their new home. They snooped cautiously in and around and under things until they felt comfortable.

"Have you decided on their names?" Amie asked.

"What do you think about Tilly and LuLu?"

"Perfect. Now how are you going to tell them apart?"

Jada held up a finger and disappeared into the bedroom. When she reappeared, she held up a little pink collar in one hand and a purple one in the other.

"Ah, so far you are staying a step ahead of them."

"Yep," Jada replied, rounding up one wiggly kitten and putting the collar on her. "I tied up the bottom of the drapes and put breakables up high."

Amie scooped up the other kitten and branded her with the purple collar. "So I dub you Tilly," she said with a kiss to the downy head. "As they grow they will develop their own unique characteristics and mannerisms, and that will make it easier, too."

"Do you think they will like it here?"

The kittens with their clumsy cuteness were wrestling and chasing and testing their climbing skills. Amie picked one kitten, clinging like Velcro, off the arm of the couch. "I think they will be just fine. But I can't say the same for your couch."

"It was well used before I got it. But maybe I can get them hooked on the playscape and scratching board. I'm picking them up tomorrow when I work on Dusty's website."

As Jada focused her attention on the kittens' antics, Amie focused on Jada—on her smile, free and unrestricted, and the joy in her eyes. She was transfixed until Jada noticed her watching.

With a hint of self-consciousness Jada asked, "What?"

Although she didn't know what response to expect, Jada *did* expect a response. What she got was an intimacy emanating from the gentle curl of Amie's lips and the gaze that caught her breath. It drew her in, wrapped itself around parts of herself that she hadn't yet identified—private, untouched parts of herself. Were they hopes, doubts or fears? She sensed that they weren't hers alone anymore. Whatever they were, she would be sharing them now.

Neither of them said anything. Jada took Amie's hand and led her to the bedroom. Light filtered through shuttered windows in the little room housing only a double bed and a dresser. Amie stopped in the narrow walkway next to the bed and pulled Jada back against her. She slid her hands around Jada's waist and kissed the tender skin below her ear.

Jada closed her eyes and leaned back against Amie's shoulder. Heat radiated through her body from the lips moving over her neck to the hands wandering across her abdomen and below. "Are you *trying* to drive me crazy?"

Amie's reply was soft next to Jada's ear. "Mmmm, hmmm." She slid one hand under the waistband of Jada's jeans and added, "If this is supposed to be just a room tour, you should tell me."

Jada answered by unfastening her jeans and lowering the zipper. Heat centered quickly, following Amie's hand sliding under the zipper and over underwear, the other under her T-shirt and sports bra to cover a small, firm breast. Slow, deliberate caresses and Amie's kisses hot at the base of her neck sent desire raging through Jada's body. With an audible breath she arched her back, placed her hand over Amie's, and pushed it further between her legs.

Amie whispered heated words between kisses to the side of Jada's face. "Oh yes, I want you." Her fingers teased under the edges of Jada's underwear, until Jada pushed them and her jeans to the floor. She turned and pulled Amie with her onto the bed, kissing her fiercely and guiding Amie's hand into the wetness.

"Now," Jada said hoarsely. "I need you now." Her only thought, her only mission. She let Amie take her past want, past need, past all conscious thought, right to the edge, the very edge. Moving with her into exquisite release and an all-consuming orgasm. She held tightly to it—holding on to the intimacy, the oneness, the remaining ripples of pleasure.

Jada ran her hands under the back of Amie's shirt, pushing it up over her head. "I want to feel you against me."

Within seconds Amie had shed her clothes and had slid naked onto the bed next to Jada. "Is this what you had in mind?"

"Yes, it is," Jada replied, her hands following the smooth lines of Amie's hip and thigh. "I'll never take without giving back."

"I know," she said softly. "I knew that the first time I kissed you."

Chapter Eleven

1971

"Do you really need to keep your room?" Ali asked. "You're rarely there, and it's a waste of money. This is your home, our home, at least until we can afford something else."

"Are you sure?" Dusty replied, rinsing the breakfast dishes and putting them in the sink. "You don't mind being my ride to work? I can walk to work from my place."

"It's not a problem," Ali said, moving around the table to embrace Dusty. "It gives us that much more time together, but even that doesn't seem to be enough." Ali met Dusty's lips, gently kissing her once, twice, then pressing a kiss to her forehead.

"Don't ever let me be a problem to you."

Ali hugged her tightly. "The problem will never be you," she said.

Although they had been meant to reassure, those words left Dusty with a slightly uneasy feeling. The feeling stayed with her while they gathered their things for the day. She tried to let the feeling fade by concentrating on their plans for a movie after work. A night out for themselves. *The Last Picture Show.* A challenge for discussion that they looked forward to. Everyone was talking about it. It had been called a creative, masterful evocation of mood, by some a rare honest depiction of sex as desperation, and a depressing look at loss of hope in a dying town. Some loved it, others hated it. But Dusty and Ali were excited to make their own assessment, and as they did with books and other movies, they would analyze it and find some relevant meaning from it. It was going to be a good evening.

Her anticipation, though, was short-lived. She followed Ali out the side door of the first-floor apartment and around the corner of the house to the small gravel parking lot. Four apartments in the well-maintained house, room for four cars in the lot. But the first sight of the lot stopped Ali short. She threw her arms up as Dusty stepped up beside her.

"*What?*"

"It's gone," Ali said. "Somebody ripped off my car."

They stood there speechless, trying to process what had happened. Finally, Ali spoke. "I guess I have to call the police."

"And I have to call the bookstore and let them know I won't be in."

Back inside the apartment, Dusty called work first. Then Ali called her manager at the office.

Dusty watched her standing there with her finger pressing the disconnect button and the handset in her hand hanging at her side. "Is everything all right?"

Ali looked up and replied, "At work, yes. I just don't want to make this call."

"You have to. They have to try to find your car."

Ali continued her hesitation. "You don't know how I hate this."

"You're not going to be talking to your father. It'll be a low-grade cop manning the report desk."

"It won't matter," she said, dialing the phone and making the call.

▽ ▽ ▽

She was more right than she knew. Two officers arrived within the hour. Ali met them in the parking lot, gave them the pertinent information and watched them write it down. It didn't take long for their purpose to become clear. The men looked at each other and smiled. Then, as the officer tucked the notepad in his pocket, he explained while his partner barely contained himself.

"There was no theft, Miss Nichols." He cocked his head in an arrogant tilt and continued. "The car is registered to Detective James Nichols and he just repossessed it."

"Repossessed? I've made every payment on that car for three years, and it's paid off. I have receipts to prove it."

"It's not your car, Miss Nichols."

She started to object again when the other officer added, "Don't waste any more of our time."

Jaw clenched tightly, Ali turned sharply and with long strides returned to the apartment. She moved briskly through the kitchen, past Dusty, and into the living room as if there were some mission's end there. Then with an abrupt turn to face Dusty, she cut the air with her hands and declared, "*This* is what we're fighting for. This is why we *must* keep fighting."

"What happened?"

"The car is registered to my father. He took it. No matter that I paid for it, paid the insurance, everything. It doesn't matter. I'm a woman, and he was the way I got that loan."

"He just *took* it?" A bewildered Dusty asked. "But why? His own daughter."

"Because he can. Because it's one more way he can show disdain for me, show his authority over me."

"So there's nothing you can do?"

"Or any woman can do," she replied, calmer now but still obviously agitated. She stood there and pleaded her case, one moment to Dusty, the next to the ceiling. "We live in a world where any man for any reason can assert their superiority over us."

"To be realistic, even if the ERA were ratified tomorrow, things won't change overnight. And some minds will never be changed."

"I know," Ali replied. "This is just me at saturation level, needing some kind of relief, needing to feel at least a little sliver of power."

"Okay, then what can we do for ourselves, by ourselves?"

"For now we need a car."

"So, what if we pool our money, could we afford a beater?"

Ali finally dropped onto the couch. "Maybe. But then we have to figure on repairs and lack of dependability. You generally get what you pay for."

"Well, let's start looking, and see what we can scrape together."

October air was crisp, light jacket weather, but still comfortable for walking to and from the bus and work. For the past two weeks Ali had navigated a rambling bus route to work from the apartment, and Dusty had walked to work from her room on the other side of town. It wasn't the getting up an hour earlier and getting home later, or setting up rides to meetings that was most disruptive to their lives. Being without a car meant that they had to live apart, except for weekends. No dinners and nights of love, no mornings with breakfast and talk of the day ahead. It was more than they were willing to sacrifice, so Dusty began investigating a combination of bus routes from the apartment, and Ali began looking for a midpoint apartment.

Meanwhile, Dusty had negotiated time to use the phone at the house where she rented a room. They had an hour every evening for conversations that carefully excluded anything too personal and were filled instead with responses of "you know." It was temporary, a situation neither of them was going to settle for. They had tasted independence and freedom, enough of it to know that they would never go back, never settle. For now, though, they had to make do.

Ali's call was right on time. Dusty lifted the handset from the phone mounted on the wall by the kitchen and stretched the long cord around the corner to sit at the dining table. Ali's voice, even at the other end of a phone call, was Dusty's rock of reassurance. It lifted her and warmed her and made her smile.

"How was your day?" Dusty asked.

"Just another day at work. Nothing much to speak of," Ali replied. "But after work, Rory saw me waiting at the bus stop. Do you remember Rory? You met him after one of the meetings at the bookstore."

"Yes, your teacher friend."

"Right. Well, he gave me a ride home and we had a chance to catch up on things. Anyway, his partner, David, is the principal at a different high school, and he has an annual fall dance thing tomorrow night and two teacher chaperones out sick. I know that this would cut into our weekend time together, but he asked me if I would help out. I would be Rory's skirt for the evening and we would help chaperone."

"Did you tell him yes?"

"No, I wanted to make sure you didn't mind first. I can say no, that we had plans. That won't affect my friendship with him at all."

"No, you should do it," Dusty replied. "Friends are important. We'll have the rest of the weekend."

She could almost hear Ali's smile as she said, "I'll make it up to you."

"Yes, you will."

A quiet chuckle from Ali and, "I can't even count how many times he's been my beard. Thank you for understanding."

"There are things we will do because there is no other choice, things we'll do because we should, and then there'll be things we do because it's right."

There was a hesitation from Ali, a thoughtful space. Then softly, "Could it be that I'm falling in love with you?"

A responding flush warmed Dusty's face. "Could you hold that thought for a more appropriate time?"

"You're blushing, aren't you?"

"How late did you say the dance will last?" She knew Ali was smiling.

"The dance ends at eleven so as soon as we can be sure every kid is out of the building, I'll call you. Rory and I will pick you up."

He was a good-looking man—sharp, athletic lines, GQ style, and a masculine stance. David Seger, principal of his first high school and, so far, successfully hiding his sexuality. His appreciation for Rory and his "date" was written all over his face.

"You two are a beautiful sight," he said as he greeted them. "You're saving my hiney tonight. I'm sorry to make this thank-you so short, but I've got a few more things to check before I open the doors. Rory will fill you in on the rules and what to watch for. *Thank you*," he said, and offered a wide white smile that had no doubt captured a few hearts, one of which was Rory's.

"Okay, rules," Rory began. "There are gates up to keep the kids from going into other parts of the building. Bathrooms are accessible in this hallway. We need to check them periodically to try to stop smoking. No making out, which we can be discretionary on. Just don't let it get heavy, and check the stage area there behind the curtains."

Ali looked around the large, nearly empty room with its walls lined with folding chairs and cringed at the memory of her own school dances. Pressured to attend by hormone-high boys and expected by the girls she hung out with. Always questioning whether dressing to look good was worth suffering unwanted attention. Even dancing to music she loved had been spoiled by boys taking liberties with sweaty hands. She wondered if there would be girls here who would seek out the refuge of the bathroom like she had—ducking in often, staying as long as possible. Maybe they would even use her ruse of practicing dance moves in front of the mirror. Maybe they were exploring the "whys" of themselves just as she had.

"Oh," Rory added, "and let me approach any group of stag guys. You don't need to endure their 'compliments.'"

"Ha," Ali replied, "I'm sure I've heard worse."

Moments later the doors opened, the lights dimmed, the music started, and a steady stream of students began to fill the auditorium. Rory in suit and tie and Ali in skirt and heels were apparent chaperones in a room of students in bell-bottoms, tunics, and miniskirts. For the next three hours they moved throughout the room without incident, disrupted some smokers, and enjoyed a Janis Joplin look-alike who jumped up on the stage to lip-synch *Piece of My Heart* and *Me and Bobby McGee*. They chatted, learned a few new dance moves, and couldn't help noticing another female chaperone who was paying more attention to David than she was to the students.

It was the first thing he addressed when they finally stood at Rory's car, free to talk.

"I'm going to have to have a skirt pretty soon," he said, "or I'm going to have a serious situation." He looked at Ali and added, "I hope you know how much you are appreciated."

"I do," she replied. "And the appreciation is mutual."

"Once Dusty gets to know us," Rory said, "do you think she would consider trading social favors?"

"I'll definitely talk with her about it."

David nodded and kissed her cheek. "Thank you again for tonight."

"Give me a minute," Rory said, handing the keys to Ali, "and then we'll go pick up your girl."

$\triangledown$ $\triangledown$ $\triangledown$

"There's a part of me," Dusty said as she followed Ali into the apartment, "that doesn't want you to undress for a while."

Ali turned with a sly grin. "Oh?"

"You're kind of taking my breath away right now." Dusty allowed her gaze to follow the svelte lines from the form-fitting sweater over the tight lines of her skirt resting inches above her knees and down shapely legs exaggerated by four-inch heels. "But you know that, don't you?"

Ali stepped toward her, leaned down and took Dusty's face in her hands. She kissed her with open, teasing touches and whispered, "I count on it."

The clothes came off with no thought of even making it to the bedroom. Skirt and hose and Dusty's jeans were stripped between whispers and kisses. The couch, just as it had that first night, was there to catch them, to cradle desire that was free to break its bounds. They loved each other, pleased each other, explored the parts of their bodies meant only for each other—all the sensitive places that spread the heat and brought such pleasure. They set their bodies free for as long as was needed to let desire for each other build to a fever pitch and explode in orgasm.

Breathless and spent, Ali wrapped herself around Dusty and snugged her close. She pressed her face against the side of Dusty's head and whispered, "Is now a good time to say that I'm falling in love with you?"

"It's perfect," Dusty whispered back.

Ali pulled the throw from the back of the couch over their cooling bodies.

"I need to ask you something," Dusty said softly.

"Uh, huh."

"I fell fast and hard. I knew that I loved you before I knew it was possible. I just wonder why you say you're 'falling' in love."

"Because I keep learning things about you that make me love you more than before."

Dusty pulled her head back to look into the beautiful eyes, vibrant even in the dimness of the room. "I love you, Ali Nichols." She nuzzled again against the curve of Ali's neck. "And I want to stay here forever."

"Oh, I haven't told you yet," Ali said. "We're going to have a car."

Dusty leaned back to make eye contact. "How?"

"David was going to trade in his car to buy a new one, but he's selling it to me on payments."

"And it will be in your name."

"Absolutely."

"You have very good friends."

"*We* have very good friends." She felt Dusty's arms tighten around her. "Are we sleeping right here tonight?"

"Mmmm, hmmm."

Chapter Twelve

"Doc didn't come with you?" Rory asked, greeting Jada at the door of the house.

"It's her week to work Saturday. You're stuck with just me today."

"Oh, no, no, no," he replied. "We are blessed. Dusty is already calling you our techno wizard."

"I haven't done anything *yet*. I hope I don't disappoint."

"I'm not worried," he said, leading her into the office off the front room. "And Dusty has either a whole lot of faith in your ability, or a lot of hope. Either way, she is very happy to have you here." He pulled a second chair up to the computer desk, and brought up the website.

Jada settled in the office chair and asked, "Should we wait for Dusty so that she can learn what we are doing?"

"Believe me when I tell you that she would rather we stick a needle in her eye. She is smart, funny, and obsessively dedicated. What she is not, is masochistic."

He made Jada laugh, and within five minutes had made her as comfortable as if she had known him for years. She looked at the soft laugh lines on the still handsome face, the gentle lean over the desk, and realized that she really liked Rory Jackson.

Rory entered the password and made the management of the website available, then straightened and said, "She's all yours. I'll help in any way that I can, but I'm here to learn, too."

"Okay, let's take a look."

As she worked, Rory took notes, and the site began to take on a fresh look and become a more easily navigated place. Eventually she reached the space where the pictures of Sweetie and Rudy were to go.

"This is where Sweetie and Rudy go, right?" Rory asked.

"Right. But I was thinking about it. You know how Sweetie ended up here, don't you?"

"Dognapped," he said and laughed.

"Yes. So what if the original owner or someone who knows him is looking for her, happens onto this site, and recognizes her?"

Rory shrugged. "What are the chances?"

She hesitated a few seconds. "I don't know. Maybe the chances are minuscule."

"But you're still worried."

Jada nodded. "I would hate for anything bad to happen."

"Okay, I have an idea," he said. "I'll meet you in the barn."

Dusty looked up from administering monthly heartworm prevention to greet Jada with a genuine smile. Seconds later she was welcomed by wiggles and a full-on Sweetie hug and little Rudy's happy dance.

"I hope you're hungry," Dusty said. "I've got a big lunch ready as soon as you and Rory are finished."

"We're almost done. We just have to take the pictures of these two stars. I was worried."

"Have no fear," Rory said, bursting into the barn, "Super Girl is here." He waved what looked like an oversized marker and added, "Who it seems can, at least temporarily, change a pittie's spots."

"And why are we doing that?" Dusty asked.

"I'm worried that someone might recognize her and let the neanderthal know where she is," Jada explained.

Dusty frowned. "What are the chances that'll happen?"

Rory started changing the star on the front of Sweetie's forehead to dark brown. "That's what I said. But we can easily make sure. And this will wash off as soon as we are finished taking the pictures." The larger white on her chest took a little longer to change, but the results were quite convincing. "Okay," he said, "let's record some cuteness."

"The website is beautiful," Dusty said, rising from the kitchen table and picking up empty dishes from in front of Jada and Rory.

Jada rose to help her clear the table. "Lunch was beautiful, Dusty. That truly is the best lasagna I've ever tasted."

"Good, because I'm sending leftovers home with you."

"And if you girls don't need me," Rory said, "I've got work to do."

"Thanks, Rory," Dusty replied. "We've got the *easy* cleanup."

They cleared the table, packed up leftovers, and loaded the dishwasher before Jada asked, "Could I ask your advice on something?"

Dusty seemed somewhat surprised but answered, "Sure. Let's sit back down. The kitchen always seems to be the place for good discussion." They settled again at the table. "What is it?"

This was the perfect person to help her, Jada was sure of it. Yet even though she had thought about it for days, she wasn't sure how to approach her. How to start? She looked into receptive eyes and just began. "I don't know what to do. There's a dog on my route who is in such bad shape, I don't know how much longer she'll live if someone doesn't step in."

"Did you report it to the Humane Society?"

Jada nodded. "And I followed up. They won't do anything."

"Did they give you a reason?"

"Just that there wasn't anything they could do. They told me to contact the police. But they just sent me back to the Humane Society."

"Did you try the Sheriff's Department?"

"Yes. They won't do anything either."

"Do you know if anyone did a visit? Sometimes they'll send someone out to investigate, and they'll talk with the owner about what needs to be done to improve the situation—like proper shelter or fresh water available. Then they check back later to see if the owner is complying."

"The Humane Society said that they sent someone out, but that there wasn't anything they could do. The owner is not complying, Dusty. I saw the dog again yesterday and she barely lifts her head, and of course no water. No one was home so I tried to get her to eat and drink." Then before Jada could stop them, the tears came, filling her eyes and quickly wiped away. "She is so thin, Dusty. I can see her bones, and she just lies there and wags her tail." The tears now streamed down her cheeks. "She's dying, and I don't know what to do."

Dusty reached for Jada's hand and held it tightly. "Okay," she said in a soothing tone, "you need to tell me everything you know about the situation. We'll figure something out. Okay?"

Jada nodded. She wiped her face and blinked back additional tears. Then she spilled the torrid details, right down to Jerry's gun experience. And Dusty listened—no signal of dismissal or fear, only a look of concern, of contemplation.

"I'm literally watching that poor dog die, and I'm helpless," Jada added. "Have you ever had to do that?"

Dusty's expression changed. The lines tightened around her eyes, forcing them into an intensity Jada hadn't seen before. And there was something else there as well, something she couldn't read—maybe sadness, or even anger. It was troubling not to know, and not to know this woman well enough to ask.

Dusty finally responded with a nod. "It's the helplessness that eats away at you. When you're searching for an answer, hoping that you'll find one, then realizing that you have to give that hope up. When there is nothing more to be done except to watch them die."

Jada had so many questions, but she sensed that just being quiet and waiting was what was needed. She wanted to know what it was that she was seeing in Dusty's eyes.

"We took turns tending to him—soothing him, feeding him, trying to keep him comfortable, and holding his hand—things many nurses were afraid to do for AIDS patients. We never left him alone." Tears welled under soft blue eyes, but she lifted her head higher and continued. "We held his hands and felt the last ounce of life leave him. So, yes, I've felt helpless."

"Who, Dusty?"

There was a moment's hesitation, a moment maybe of questioning trust or of overriding a lifelong caution. Just enough time for Jada to wonder if it was a question too personal, an invasion that was unjustified by her desire to know more about this woman.

And then, "A good friend."

"Oh, Dusty, I'm so sorry."

Seemingly more at ease now, Dusty replied, "Sometimes it seems so long ago, and other times it seems like just yesterday."

The revelations were seamless, fitting perfectly with who Jada had hoped her to be. But there was so much more.

"So let's try to save a dog's life," Dusty said with a look of determination. "Shall we?"

The plan was preceded by Jada driving Dusty out to see exactly what the physical situation was like. On the way she talked about her concern with the connection to the militia. Law enforcement was well aware of that connection, and it wouldn't take much, Dusty offered, to convince the

Humane Society to avoid confrontation if he greeted them in the driveway with a gun. "They're weighing the threat to human life against the death of a dog," she said.

"So, am I going too far? Risking too much?" Jada asked.

"Slow down when you get to the house so that I can get a good look."

Past an abandoned overgrown field, Jada slowed the car. "If you see anyone, turn and look straight ahead and gradually increase your speed," Dusty directed.

"Okay," Jada replied. "No one yet. There's the dog, lying under that tailgate leaning against the house. Can you see her?" The dog lifted her head at the sound of the car. "She's still alive, Dusty."

Dusty nodded, her eyes surveying the house and surroundings. "What does he drive?"

"A blue truck. That other truck there is junk. It's always in the same spot, flat tire, dirty windshield."

"Doesn't look like he's here then."

"But that doesn't mean that the kid isn't here. There's no way to know when *he's* here."

"Right," Dusty replied. "We'll have to do this late at night."

"Then we're going to do it?" Jada was partly relieved and partly surprised. It seemed more daunting now that it could be more than a thought or a hope. "How are we going to do it?"

"Keep driving, so I can figure out where to park."

The car crept slowly past the house and a wooded area adjacent to it until Dusty said, "There, that flat space. It looks like it used to be a drive to that field back there. Okay, about three in the morning I'll stop the car there, open the back and leave it running. I should be able to get the dog, put her in the car and get out of here without waking anyone up."

"You?" Jada asked. "By yourself?"

"No sense in both of us risking our hineys."

"So you're going to sneak from the car to the house, lift

the dog and carry it to the car, maybe even have to run, put her in the back and then get in the car—all that before a bullet hits your butt."

"Do you have a better plan?"

"Well, we need to come up with something better than that."

"We?"

"Yes, we," Jada replied. "No offense, but I have younger legs. And even with that, we'll have to do this a lot quicker." She turned around in the next neighbor's drive. "I have an idea." Jada drove slowly past the house again. "What if you drive, let me out right by that tree at the end of the driveway and stay right there? I won't have as far to go and we can get out of here quicker."

"You're sure you want to do this?"

"Yes."

"Okay. I will pick you up at two-thirty. Wear dark clothing and a hood. Your hair is too recognizable."

Chapter Thirteen

Amie didn't know. In all the sharing they'd done about their day, Jada couldn't bring herself to tell her about the planned late-night caper. It hadn't seemed right—not yet. There were too many "maybes" stopping her. Maybe Amie would have talked her out of it, convinced her to have another go at the organizations. Maybe not telling her was circumventing their first argument. Or maybe it would be neither of those, and Amie would be full on board and support her decision. But she didn't know, and Jada wasn't ready to find out—not tonight.

At precisely two-thirty a.m., Dusty, hair tucked up under a ball cap, picked her up in a dark blue SUV. "Here we go," she said, as Jada climbed into the front seat. "Let's hope that he sleeps like a hibernating bear and snores like one, too."

Jada laughed, but it was tinged with a nervous energy. She marveled at Dusty's calm confidence. The image of a starving dog waiting for her only hope for survival was Jada's only hope to keep her focus on the mission and not on the risk.

"You okay?" Dusty asked.

"Yeah, I'm good." Jada met the question in Dusty's eyes in the dim light of the car. "Really. We have to try to save her."

"Yes, we do."

$$\triangledown \quad \triangledown \quad \triangledown$$

As they approached the house, Dusty shut off the car lights and drove slowly past the house to the spot on the other side of the tree. Jada pulled up her hood and quietly slipped from the car while Dusty went to the back and lifted the hatch.

Jada crept across the driveway, her eyes adjusting to the dark, her heart pounding so hard that she could hear it. "Please be okay," she whispered, nearing where she hoped the dog still was. "*Please.*"

All was dark and quiet, no lights or signs of life in the house. A slight breeze cooled her face, already sweaty under the hood. But as Jada crept closer to the tailgate, pleading under her breath for the dog not to whine, the whole area was suddenly flooded in light. Jada dropped quickly to a crouch as the dog raised her head. Her heart pounded in fear. How long did she have? Did the light wake him? How hard did he sleep?

The dog began to whine as she reached around the dog's back and under her front legs to pull her from under the tailgate. "Shhhh, it's okay, girl," she whispered close to the dog's head. "Shhh." She struggled to get in a position to lift her while the dog struggled weakly to stand on her own. Finally able to get a good hold around her chest and stomach, Jada lifted her and stood.

But as soon as she was upright she heard sound coming from the house. A door? With fear kicking her adrenaline into full flight mode, she struggled to run with the weight of the dog. "Come on," she encouraged her legs, "Come on."

"Hey," came a shout from the house. "What the hell?"

Jada's grip on the dog began to slip, but the decision was made; she would not let her go. She stopped, rested the weight of the dog on her thighs and reestablished her grip. Just a little way to go; she could make it.

Then, louder this time, "Hey, what the hell are you doing?"

He was on the porch, Jada heard the screen door slam shut. And a sound. Was it a gunshot?

Dusty was ready behind the wheel as Jada dropped the dog into the back of the car and closed the hatch. Seconds later she was sliding into the front seat when a bullet shattered the door window before she could pull it shut.

The car lurched onto the road. Lights off, Dusty floored the accelerator and sped into the darkness.

"Shit!" Jada exclaimed. *"Shit! Shit!"*

"Are you hit?"

"No, just fucking scared."

"Just tell me where to turn."

"I can't tell," Jada said. "A little farther."

Dusty flipped on the lights.

"There," Jada said, "right there."

Dusty made the turn and doused the lights again. She looked behind them in time to see lights had entered the road they had just left. Again, Dusty floored the accelerator, racing down the dark road and depending on Jada's recognition of landmarks.

"That light, high on the pole up there on the left," she said, "it's a farm. The turn is just past it."

Dusty used the lights again to see the turn, then switched them off as they started down another dark road. She checked the mirror to see if there were lights behind them. Nothing. But she sped as fast as possible in the dark. "How far now?"

"Another mile or so."

"Watch for lights behind us, I have to put the parking lights on so I can stay on the road."

Jada continually checked until she felt they were close. "Slow down a little," she said. "There'll be a big rustic sign, no higher than the car, at the entrance to the park." She watched anxiously for it. "You'll have to use the lights in the park. The road winds all over the place."

Dusty reached over and placed her hand on Jada's arm.

"You're shaking," she said. "Take a couple of deep breaths. We're going to be okay."

Jada followed her advice, breathing deeply while her heart resisted the effort. "We must be close."

A few yards later, the parking lights caught the log-framed sign, and Dusty made the turn into the park. With full lights now, it was clear why they were needed. A narrow paved road wound through large growths of trees and ambled alongside a rambling river.

"Well, you were not exaggerating," Dusty said. "And," she added with a look in the mirror, "if those *were* his lights we saw, we've lost him."

"This is a huge county park, and it'll take us back to the main road to the animal hospital."

"You feeling better?"

"Some, yes," Jada replied. "But I'll feel a lot better once we get this poor girl some help." She looked into the back but could tell nothing except that the dog didn't seem to have moved.

"Yes, me, too."

Dusty rang the bell at the animal hospital's emergency door while Jada checked on the dog. At the sight of her rescuer she began to whine and did her best to push up onto her front legs. "Yes," Jada said, stroking her head, "I know you're trying."

"Here, let me get her inside," said a young male staff employee. He offered the top of his hand before gently moving to stroke her face, then wrapped his arms around her chest and butt and lifted her from the car.

They followed him into the building and talked with the doctor on call as he began his examination. The story was that they had found her at the edge of a parking lot and that Dusty would be the contact for her care.

106

"We'll get her hydrated and see if she'll eat some soft food, and basically get her comfortable," he said. "We'll do some tests and see what we're dealing with. I'll contact you as soon as we have some results," he said to Dusty.

"I have a place for her," she replied, "if we can get her on the mend."

"We'll do our best by her," he promised.

The sense of hope and relief Jada felt was evident as she collapsed in the passenger seat. Dusty laughed softly and dropped her head back against the headrest.

"You, my friend," Jada began, "are one helluva driver. I cannot believe how calm you were."

"This isn't my first go-around. But you knowing those roads made this so much easier."

"You've done this before?"

"With even more valuable cargo on board." Dusty started the car and circled the building to the exit.

Jada's patience lasted only so long. When there was no indication that Dusty was going to offer the rest of the story, she said, "I probably have a better than average imagination, but you just can't leave me hanging like that. Remember, this *is my* first go-around."

"I'll admit," Dusty said, pulling onto the main road, "back then I shook as badly as you did—but I was driving. I thought for sure I'd end up killing us before *he* could."

When there was another hesitation, Jada interjected, "Oh no you don't. Don't even question what to tell me. We just stole a dog together."

"Rescued," Dusty corrected. "We rescued a dog together."

"Right," Jada offered with a broad smile.

"Okay, here's the good, the bad, and the ugly of it. The good," she said, her eyes straight ahead and pensive, "was a woman I loved more than anything on this earth and a life with her I hadn't even dreamed of. But as good as the good was, the bad was equally bad. Her father hated that she publicly fought for equal rights. He hated our lifestyle. He hated me. Everything that he could do to make our lives miserable, he did. And as a detective there wasn't much he couldn't do."

Dusty checked her mirrors as she spoke, maybe out of habit, maybe more. "One night he called the apartment. He'd been drinking and told Ali that I'd better be gone for good before he got there. Ali didn't scare easily—she'd grown up with him trying to control her—but it scared *me*. She told him to go to hell, and he replied that he was on his way and would put a bullet between my eyes. If he had threatened her, I'm sure she would have stood her ground. But it was me."

Jada listened as if she was hearing an episode of *Dateline* or *48 Hours*. It seemed so remote, a real-life story that couldn't possibly have happened to someone she knew. She listened, spellbound.

"I cut my teeth that night," Dusty continued. "We grabbed purses and keys and left. Ali pushed the keys into my hand and told me to drive while she hid in the backseat. She thought it out so quickly. If he saw me driving away alone, he would think that he had won. And by the time he found that Ali was not in the apartment, we'd have a head start. And we did. We passed him coming down the block, and we stayed ahead of him. Ali figured that since this was a personal, alcohol-inspired mission he wouldn't involve his police pals. The rest of our flight depended on that. I drove through neighborhoods and parking lots in an erratic path, staying away from the main city arteries."

It was playing out like a movie in Jada's mind. In the movie a fresh-faced young Dusty gripped the wheel tightly, nervously checking her mirrors, and fighting the internal quiver that Jada herself had felt tonight. She tried to envision Ali—was she slight like Dusty, fair or dark? She was leaning over the back of the driver's seat, her arms around Dusty's shoulders, telling her that everything was going to be okay. It was Jada's painful, tightening wish that that had happened, that real life had paralleled her movie. She wanted to know that the strength of Ali's arms had calmed the quiver, that the sound of her voice against Dusty's ear had quelled the fear, fostered her strength.

"We kept winding our way down back roads and staying off I-75 to get to the Ohio border. I didn't breathe normally for hours."

It wasn't until Dusty stopped talking that Jada realized that they were sitting in front of her house. "Oh," she said, "please don't stop now. You have to tell me the rest."

"Do you know what time it is?" Dusty asked, checking her watch. "You have Sunday off. I don't."

"I don't mean to be selfish. But I'll be thinking about you and Ali until I know what happened. Look, I was going to tell you this anyway, but I'll be out tomorrow and work all day."

"You're still going to get the Reader's Digest version."

"I'll take it."

Dusty relaxed against the driver's door. "We stayed at a motel in Ohio, called Rory and David the next day and told them we weren't coming back. Rory had a key, so they collected our things from the apartment and as soon as we got a place in Dayton, they brought them down to us. Rory loaned us money until we got new jobs."

"I knew I liked him the minute I met him."

"Was it the fist bump?" Dusty asked with a smile.

Jada laughed. "An exclamation point."

"He's a special soul." She looked down for a moment. Jada waited. "We came back to Michigan when David got sick." She met Jada's eyes with a seriousness that convinced Jada not to ask further. "That's all for tonight. Okay?"

Jada returned the seriousness she saw, replying, "You trusting me with parts of your life means a lot to me. I hope you know that."

"It was a long time ago. In many ways a different world."

"And in other ways, not so different."

"I guess I can still rock a getaway car."

"You can indeed," Jada replied with a smile.

"And you're not a bad dog rescuer, I must admit." Dusty squared herself behind the wheel again.

"One more thing," Jada said. "The kid said that his mother used to call the dog Brandy. I didn't want to use her name. You know, it would make it so much more personal, and so much harder if she doesn't make it."

"I know."

"But I can't help it," Jada admitted, "I want to use her name."

"Then Brandy it is."

Chapter Fourteen

1985

"It is surprising that the president could remain silent as 6,000 Americans died, that he could fail to acknowledge the epidemic's existence. Perhaps his staff felt he had to, since many of his New Right supporters have raised money by campaigning against homosexuals."

Rep. Henry Waxman (D-CA), *The Washington Post*, 1985

A month. A month to grieve, to accept loss, to decide what direction your life would take. It wasn't nearly enough, they all knew it.

Dusty let herself into Rory's apartment, just as she or Ali had done for a month now. She expected to find him in bed this late in the day, unshowered, unshaven and unnourished. The routine was the same each time, coax and resist, coax and relent. And although the resistance at times was quite convincing, no one believed that he didn't want to live. It was the quality of his life that concerned them. Family was uninformed and too far away; calls from male friends went unanswered. The only blessing to the timing of David's death was that it was July—a small window of time to grieve privately without having to hope for bereavement leave for a "close friend."

There were few blessings to hang onto, though, until today. Dusty was headed toward the bedroom as usual when she heard, "Which Sister of Mercy is here?" He stood in the doorway of the kitchen, fresh and clean shaven, dressed in jeans and a bright white T-shirt.

"What a pretty sight you are," Dusty said in greeting.

He handed Dusty a cup of coffee and pulled out a chair at the table for her. "I got up today," he said, folding into a chair, "and I could smell myself. I could feel the acids eating at the lining of my stomach. And I saw the scruff of growth on my face—for the first time since . . ." He sipped his coffee, elbows resting on the table. "And I thought," with a tilt of his head, "a lady doesn't do this to her friends."

Dusty's laugh was easy and light with relief. "I'm so glad you're back. We've been worried that we were losing our Rory, too."

"I've been trying to think, but it hasn't been easy when part of my mind is sure that this is all a nightmare and that everything will be okay as soon as I wake up. I need to figure out what parts of me are still me and what is gone."

She watched the deep-set eyes struggling with the sadness. "We're right here, whatever you find."

"That means more than you will ever imagine."

"Well, besides Ali," she replied, "you're my best girlfriend." It was enough to get a sly smile and the girlish turn of his head that made *her* smile. "Which means," she added, "you have to tell me when I can help."

"You and Ali have already done more than I could ask for."

But she sensed in his tone, in his eyes, there *was* something. "Ali has an interview after work, so I have a few hours if you don't mind me hanging around."

"Would you want to go with me to David's apartment? I have to do it sooner or later."

And he surely did not want to do it alone, not yet.

Nothing had been touched since David's death. The apartment looked as though he would come around the corner with his usual greeting and offer them his latest sweet treat. They were about to destroy even that impossibility.

"Let's just start with gathering your things and putting them in the car," Dusty suggested. Ease into it. It was going to get painful.

He packed a duffel with clothes and toiletries and handed them dutifully to Dusty.

"I put boxes in the kitchen," she said. "Let's do that next."

They emptied the refrigerator and a couple of cabinets. Dusty watched him closely, watching for a sign that said they'd done enough today. So far, though, he was focused on the task at hand.

"Who's your girl interviewing with?" he asked when Dusty returned from a trip to the car.

"Dodds and Drake," she replied. "They have a paralegal position open. She's pretty excited."

"That's where she worked before."

Dusty nodded. "She did secretarial work then, but she was always reading and learning and doing extra work for them. So, when she contacted them about coming back to work, they told her to interview for the open position."

"A smart man will hire her."

"That's what I'm thinking," Dusty said. "She was already doing research on some of their smaller cases. I really hope she gets this."

"And when she does," he replied, "I'm taking our—my— best girlfriends to Detroit's best five-star restaurant to celebrate."

He recovered from the slip easier than Dusty expected. "Well, you know we'd never turn *that* down. Damn, that's a dress-to-the-nines event."

"Managed by one of the boys. It's exquisite."

"You've got a date," Dusty said. "Now all Ali has to do is turn on her magnetic charm and remind them of how smart she is. Okay, I'm taking this box out to the car."

When she returned from taking a second box out, Dusty found Rory in the bedroom sitting on the end of the bed. He was clutching a white sweatshirt to his chest, and when he lifted his head, his eyes, a hardened hazel, defied the tears making their way down his cheeks. "I'm so angry!" he shouted. "So goddamn angry! I want to stand in the middle of the street and scream it to the world—what right do you have? What goddamn right? I want to scream it, Dusty. I want to scream it till it scorches my lungs and takes my last breath."

He clenched his fists, jammed them hard against the edge of the bed, threw his head back and screamed, "Whyyyy? Goddamn, someone tell me *why!*" He grabbed the sweatshirt again and clutched it tightly to his chest with both hands. Tears washed over cheeks quivering with still unleashed anger.

He rocked back and forth, buried his face in the sweatshirt, and continued to rock. Dusty dropped onto the edge of the bed beside him, tears filling her own eyes, unsure of how to help him. This was the man who made everyone else feel better, whose gestures and humor made you giggle no matter how pissed or upset you were. That smile, that barely noticeable curl of the corners, said that he knew his own magic—that he had stolen your distress and, for a time, hidden it away. She needed use of his magic right now. If only she could . . .

Rory lifted his head again, looking to the anonymity of the ceiling. In a tone that was lower, but still firm and tinged with anger, he said, "They *want* us dead. Every one of us—every fag, every queer, every queen. All of us." He turned to look directly into Dusty's eyes. "That's it, isn't it?"

Everything pointed to him being right. Reagan hadn't even breathed the word, and no money had been allocated for research or treatment. It was wiping out an abomination. Why stop it? "Well," Dusty began, her arm around Rory's shoulders, "that would leave one stale, ugly world. Who the hell is going to get the next generation out of shoulder pads and Members Only Jackets, save them from Fawcett hair, and—"

"It will be ugly. They have no idea. And they'll deserve every god-awful leg warmer, acid wash, maxi-dress moment of it. May they live forever in monochromatic dorm design rooms with mass-produced posters hanging on the walls and Led Zeppelin ringing in their ears. Someday maybe they'll miss us."

"If every gay man withheld their services for a week, they'd miss you now."

"And we'd out ourselves to an even faster annihilation. By the time they figure out what we contribute it will be too late."

"I still wish you could do it," Dusty replied. "I wish women could do it—even for a day, even just the feminists—they'd pee their drawers to see how much of the world we could shut down."

Calmer now, Rory replied, "Think what would happen if we joined forces."

"*That* would be a force, wouldn't it?"

She wrapped her arms around him and kissed the side of his head. He dropped his face into the sweatshirt and just let her hold him.

"Okay," she said softly, "we've done enough for today. Let's go back to our apartment and wait for Ali."

He nodded, still holding the sweatshirt to his face.

She squeezed her arms around him. "Come on, let's see if some smart man hired our girl."

He lifted his head and nodded again. "I'm taking this with me," he said. "It was his favorite."

"Has Ali's father bothered you since you've been back?"

"Not so far," Dusty replied. "I don't think he knows where we are. We chose this place because it's a bigger building and it's on the other side of town. We're using a PO box for our address and we still have our Ohio driver's licenses."

"There is no excuse for that kind of hatred," Rory said. "Hatred that threatens your life is criminal. At least David's family just didn't want anything to do with him. And mine is naïve and keeps trying to marry me off."

"Their reactions aren't as scary, but they're still hurtful," she said. "And that reminds me, I am going to make payments to you for David's car. You're not giving it to me."

"No, Dusty, no one from his family's going to claim it, and I don't need it. It's yours."

"It's mine on a payment plan, don't argue with—"

"Hey!" came Ali's voice as she burst through the door. "I have champagne!" Then she rounded the corner of the living room and saw Rory. "Ohhh, are you a beautiful sight," she exclaimed as Rory stood. She wrapped him in a tight embrace and added, "I'm so glad you're here."

"You got it, didn't you?" Dusty asked.

"I did," she replied, kissing Dusty soundly. Then holding up the champagne bottle, she added, "And we're drinking to it."

Minutes later they were clinking glasses and smiling and toasting Ali's advancement. Moments of much needed happiness that lifted their spirits and soon morphed naturally into a shared time of reflection.

"You've wanted this for a long time, haven't you?" Rory asked.

"I've wanted law school for a long time," Ali replied, "but this is a good step. And," she said, looking intently into

Dusty's eyes, "I hope the increased salary will make your decision easier."

The look was commitment, love for the long haul, and Dusty recognized it, cherished it. She loved this woman more than she could say.

"Hello?" Rory interrupted.

Dusty broke eye contact to answer. "I have an opportunity to work at the veterinary hospital on the other side of town, but it would be a pay cut from managing the bookstore."

"But it's also your chance to do what you weren't able to do before. Maybe we can put some money aside for you to take classes." Ali's tone was hopeful, encouraging. "Plus, if they know you're serious about veterinary school, they may have a program that will help pay for your education. It's worth checking into it."

"If that's your dream," Rory added, "then you need to do it."

Dusty took a deep breath. "I'd sort of given up on it. But if you both—"

"We do," they replied in unison.

"And that calls for another toast," Ali said, refilling their glasses. "To Dr. Logan."

"That sounds so strange, and impossible," Dusty replied. "But I won't know unless I try."

"Yes!" Ali declared with another clink of their glasses.

"Okay," Rory began as he settled his thin frame back into the overstuffed chair," with all this deciding and convincing going on, I could use a little of it." His brow was pressed into a deep line above his nose.

"We're at your disposal, Mister," Ali replied.

"I can't believe that I am contemplating something that could get me fired."

Ali looked surprised. "Neither can I."

"I've been thinking about it ever since David got sick.

117

I've *always* wanted to teach. I love teaching history. I love kids—their potential, their energy, all the possibilities and paths of their launch into adulthood that I can help them navigate. And I'm good at it."

"There's no doubt about that," Dusty interjected. "I'd say that being Teacher of the Year last year proves it."

"But I loved David, too. We always protected our careers—separate apartments, gay bars only in Toledo, and any other socializing was with a skirt, thanks to dear friends."

"So what are you contemplating?" Ali asked.

"Too many people are dying," he said, "and something has to be done. The government won't help. They won't study it or anything; it's just a gay man's disease. It's up to us."

"What are you saying?" asked Dusty.

"I need to find a way to help."

Ali added the obvious. "Without them firing the Teacher of the Year."

Rory nodded. "If they suspect I'm gay, I'll be fired in a nanosecond. There is so much I want to do. I can give money to the efforts to understand and treat this horrible disease, but what's most important is educating the public—what it is, what it does, how it's spread. It's the only way to stop it."

"Write about it," Ali said. "Use a pen name and write about everything they're finding out about it. Write articles or essays. And send them everywhere—magazines, newspapers, health departments."

"Colleges, high schools," added Dusty. "They need to include it in their curriculums."

Rory listened, brow knitted intently. "Never considered myself much of a writer."

"Write it like you would teach it." Ali said.

Chapter Fifteen

"When were you going to tell me?" Amie asked, her only greeting as Jada entered the apartment.

The question had been expected—not the abruptness and the hard-edged tone of it, but the question itself was no surprise. Jada's reactive frown prompted a second question.

"Or *weren't* you going to tell me?" Amie returned the frown.

Jada remained standing stiffly in the archway of the living room. "Are you talking about Brandy?" A lame, no doubt irritating filler—an ineffective speck of time in order to form an answer that would soften the tension.

Amie cocked her head. "Really?" she replied. "It's been almost a week and not a word. Instead, I was left to believe that she was a dog Dusty had rescued—until today when Chad said that the FedEx driver had brought her in and I put two and two together. She's the militia dog, isn't she?"

"Yes," she replied without hesitation.

"You told me you were going to try the sheriff and the organizations again."

"I did, Amie. No one was willing to help."

"So you went to Dusty Logan for advice? Why didn't you come to *me*?"

Jada shrugged. "Maybe because I knew how you would react."

"Which is how?"

"Would you have supported me rescuing her? Would you have helped me?"

"To do something illegal? To put yourself at risk? Why would I do something like that to someone I love, someone I thought was serious about a relationship? Why would you expect me to do that?"

"Because I thought that you felt the same as I do. I thought all life was important to you."

"All life *is* important, of course it's important. But—"

"She was dying, Amie."

"And I'm supposed to be okay with sending you into a situation where you could be shot at."

"I *was* shot at."

Amie threw her arms in the air. "Oh, good God! That's my *point*," she said and turned away abruptly. An awkward silence followed while Jada watched Amie's back. There was an unmistakable sense of frustration, and maybe anger. She waited, more sure by the moment that there was nothing she could say that would resolve it.

Amie turned again to face her, hands on her hips. "You could have died, Jada. You could have *died*."

Still, silence from Jada.

"And Dusty was okay with that? She was okay that by taking her advice, following her lead, that you could have been killed? That's beyond me, Jada. Beyond my comprehension."

"It was *my* decision," Jada replied. "She would have done it by herself, but I couldn't let her. *I* decided to do it."

"And you'd do it again, wouldn't you?"

The sudden rise of defiance was unexpected. "Yes, I would," Jada said. She stood her ground without offering a defense, and without thought of the personal cost.

There was another long silence. They stared across the tension-charged distance between them. Amie seemed hesitant to respond, her eyes locked on Jada's as if the next words held too heavy a burden. Finally, "I don't know what to say. I don't even know what I'm feeling right now."

"It sounds like you're angry—angry at me for being me. That's what it sounds like."

"Yes," Amie returned, "you're right. Part of it *is* anger. The rest I don't know. I don't know what you want from a relationship. I guess I don't know what *I* want."

"So what are we doing then? Just filling lonely nights? Satisfying sexual needs?" Jada shrugged her shoulders. "What?"

"If that's what we're doing, it's not what I want."

"And if you think that's what we've been doing, then maybe I'm not the one you need." Without waiting for Amie to respond, Jada left the apartment.

She drove around town, obeying traffic signals by rote, letting the harshness and anger of their words replay themselves over and over. She hated it, hated the sound of her own words, of Amie's. She searched for why, fought the anger, and drove. Yet, no matter how far or how long she drove, emotions kept their stranglehold on clear thought.

There'd be no sleep if she went home—only pacing and self-doubt, and questions with only confusion as an answer. She needed to talk it out and hear trusted advice. But at this time in her life, the choices were limited. Her mother, maybe, but Jada hated to disturb her evening. Her sister— older, detached, and very judgmental of her lifestyle—had never really been an option. And longtime friend Elaine now had her hands full with three little ones.

Jada pulled the car into an empty parking lot and dialed Dusty's number.

Dusty met her at the door in jeans and denim shirt, sleeves rolled to the elbows. "Come on," she said, "let's walk and talk."

"Thank you," Jada began. "I didn't want to disrupt your evening, but I need to talk with someone."

"Of course you do, and who better than the one who got you into this in the first place."

"No, don't feel that way. I'm an adult. I'm responsible for my own decision. I just need perspective."

"Perspective on love," Dusty said and followed with a subtle smile. "Is there such a thing?"

"Right now, for me—no."

They walked slowly around the west side of the house and along a path of wood chips as the pink and blue tint of the day's last light silhouetted a border of maples. The electric sound of the cicadas filled the air.

"Are you in love with her?" Dusty asked.

Jada nodded. "But I'm not so sure that she feels the same way."

"What makes you say that?"

"If she did, wouldn't she accept me for who I am?"

"Including putting yourself at risk?"

Jada nodded again.

"You know, you can't really know who another person is until they have a chance to show you."

The end of the path opened onto the bank of a large pond. The water reflected the brilliance of the setting sun, now half an orb slipping below the far bank and spilling a bright red-orange glow across the pond.

The women settled on large flat rocks nestled into the side of the bank. "This is beautiful, Dusty."

"Mother Nature is still a woman who can take my breath away."

Jada smiled and noticed the colorful reflection in Dusty's eyes. Yes, Mother Nature, her beauty, her complexity was a blessing, Jada thought. But she wondered if Dusty realized how much of a blessing *she* was. Offering advice, support, available to the needs of someone she barely knew. She was a blessing that Jada had certainly not expected.

"You know," Dusty began in a soft tone, "Ali told me for twenty-one years that she was falling in love with me." The smile that followed was a gentle lift of the corners of her mouth, introspective and private. She noticed the questioning press of Jada's brow and added, "I didn't understand at first either. Me? I fell fast—and hard, before I even knew what it meant. But for Ali, she said that she kept learning things all along that made her love me more each time."

"Twenty-one years."

"This year," Dusty added, "would have been forty-six. I never wanted anyone else, or anything except what our life was together."

"I thought that finding someone for life was only possible for people like my parents. I've never known anyone like you. Everything I thought and wondered about was based on what I saw, what I experienced. You must think I'm—"

"Naïve? That's nothing to be ashamed of," Dusty said. "Part of you not knowing what's possible is the fault of people like myself. Most were silent and stayed in the shadows. For couples to amass that many years together they had to have begun their relationships during a time when exposure meant serious consequences—loss of family, career, opportunity. Too many of them still live in silence. Without Ali, I have to share that guilt. I went back into the shadows and stayed there."

"I know about Edie Windsor," Jada recalled. "I know about her struggle, but not about her life."

"Have you ever read *Lesbian Woman* by Phyllis Lyon and Del Martin?"

Jada shook her head. "No."

"Then I'll send it home with you if you promise to read it."

"Of course I will."

"It was incredible how those two women, after nineteen years together, were able to make so many of us realize that we *are* normal. When the rest of the world considered us mentally ill and in many ways just tragic beings, their example of life together was a life buoy. They showed us that commitment, and love, and happiness were possible—and normal—a life that was not only possible, but one we should expect."

"So I should be dreaming bigger."

"You should dream your own dream. Talk to Amie and find out if that dream includes her. But you have to believe that everything you're willing to fight for is possible. Something I had lost sight of until now."

Chapter Sixteen

1989

R-E-S-P-E-C-T

"You're right," Ali began, taking Dusty's hand and eyeing a table next to the mezzanine railing, "we desperately need time in our own world."

A microcosm of a world held only in wishful thinking, Café GiGi checked off a good number of boxes. Once inside its doors, it was a safe space, filled with lesbians, and protected from harassment and damage to cars in the parking lot by a well-compensated beat cop. It was furnished and maintained as well as any mainstream night club with café tables and cushioned chairs, a full-length bar, and a well-placed dance floor.

Despite the cigarette smoke, which regardless of whether or not she drank always resulted in a headache, Dusty loved it here. This was indeed their world. Here the looks from others didn't bring fear of condemnation or confrontation. There was no need to feel uncomfortable or to avoid eye contact. Here looks asked, "Do I know you?" "Where do I know you from?" "Can I get to know you?" This is where closing the loop was possible and safe.

Dusty looked around as they waited for their drinks. The loop had closed for many of the women there. She and Ali knew their names, where they lived and worked. For some their mannerisms and attire made them obvious in the larger community; others blended in without much effort. Yet whether blending or not, every woman here needed this place, cherished this place.

Dusty moved her chair closer, and Ali put her arm around her shoulders and kissed the side of her head. "This is so important," Dusty said.

"Spending time here?"

"No, no, more than that. There are probably as many reasons for being here as there are women here tonight. Beyond that, I mean being able to touch each other, look at each other like this. It's so different than at home in private," she said, looking around at women at the other tables comfortable in casual intimacy. "It's a kind of freedom, isn't it?"

"I think it's even more than that," Ali replied. "I think it's a validation of normalcy. To be able to show affection in front of others, to see them doing the same makes us as normal as any straight couple. Each of us, for as long as we are here in this place, is validating each other."

She was right. Dusty slid her hand around Ali's waist and leaned her head against her shoulder as they watched the women on the dance floor. Words, verbal affirmation, weren't necessary. Not here. No one had to declare it; it just was, normal. "Do you think it will ever be like this for us in the rest of society?"

"Are you doubting our efforts at equality?"

"Not the need for them," Dusty said, sitting up and looking at Ali. "I know we have to keep fighting—so that at least on the books they can't discriminate against us. But, realistically . . ."

"Well, we have two strikes against us: we're women and we're lesbians. Changing the attitudes of so many people—

people like my own family—isn't going to be easy. And in some cases, not even possible. But to settle for the way it is now is not acceptable."

"Sometimes I get so tired, though. I know you do, too, but you just won't admit it."

"Maybe that's the universe telling us that it's a battle that has to be fought, no matter how tired we are. It's that vital. It comes down to not wanting to live or die as a second-class citizen."

"That's why I hope this place is always here. There are no second-class citizens here," Dusty said, sipping her piña colada and entertaining wishful thoughts. "You know," she began as she made another passing glance around the bar, "even with just the women we know here we'd have the nucleus of our own community. We could start our own state."

The thought, as improbable as it was, made Ali smile. "Danny works construction building houses," she mused.

"Judy's a financial advisor. Ellen's a nurse. Sally's a teacher."

"Chris drives a truck and does all her own mechanics, and both Lisa and Lynn are ex-military."

"And those are just the ones we know," Dusty added.

"We're dreaming," Ali replied, "trying to find an easier way."

"I know. But just the idea makes me feel good."

"Yep. But for now," Ali said, pushing her chair back, "we have GiGi's, good women, and good music." She stood and reached out her hand. "Come on and dance with me."

Right here, right now, Dusty Logan was as normal as they come. Held in the arms of the woman she loved more than life itself, and surrounded by a dance floor full of women just like herself, she was honest and true and normal.

Ali's arms, wrapped around Dusty's back, held her firmly against the length of her body. The familiar strength and sultry movement joined them together, fused in a welcome, expected heat. She loved how Ali moved, loved how easily her own body matched the press of her thigh and the motion of her hips. They continued moving slowly to the sound of Etta James singing their affirmation, "At Last." Ali whispered softly against Dusty's ear. "You are mine. And we are in heaven."

And they were. Dusty had never had a doubt. The words were true all those years ago, and as true now as they were then. They had no license for their love, signed and notarized, recognized by the state, by society. Their commitment to each other had been made in time, witnessed by only those trusted and close. It had been made day by day, month by month, and year by year.

Dusty pressed her lips to the smooth curve of Ali's neck. "I love you," she said, and pressed another kiss below Ali's ear.

Ali smiled against the side of Dusty's head, leaned them to the left and then turned them to the right into a tight circle. "And I love *you*, Dusty Logan. More than you'll ever know."

"I think you should keep trying to show me."

"I will, but it may take years," Ali replied with a kiss at the end of the song that sealed her promise.

The trip back to their table took a bit longer than usual. There was always catching up to do from table to table. Health concerns for some friends, job changes for others, and for those elbow to elbow in the equality movement. Encouragement—Ali gave it out like candy laced with a hard shot of Johnny Walker. Dusty marveled at how tired, worried lines were transformed into a confident defiance on the faces of those who counted on Ali's word.

Gena Harris held Ali's arm throughout their conversation. She and her partner were watching closely all movement on the discrimination front, hoping for some workplace protection for the gay and lesbian community. Gena's job as a public school teacher was always in jeopardy, threatened by the exposure of who she loved.

"Has your firm decided," Gena asked, still holding Ali's arm and her attention, "whether they'll take on the Richardson case?"

"Yes," Ali replied. "I saw the memo Thursday that they took the case. And yesterday they assigned it to me. I finally have something that I can sink my teeth into."

"I can't think of anyone better," Gena said. "I've been waiting ever since you passed the bar for them to give you something that will make a difference."

"She's been biding her time and paying her dues," Dusty added. "She's earned this chance."

"Well, the firm will get a lot of publicity, but I'm sure none of the senior attorneys were raising their hand and jumping up and down for this one."

Gena's partner was more pragmatic and less hopeful. "It's going to be a tough argument, isn't it?"

"It shouldn't be," Ali replied. "But, yes, it will be tough. It will take a decision that interprets the coverage of the word 'sex' in the 1976 Civil Rights Law. Does it include and cover sexual orientation?"

"I know one thing," Gena said with a squeeze of Ali's arm, "and that is, if it can be done, I believe you can do it."

"I appreciate your confidence," Ali said. "You have my promise to give it the best I've got."

Something no one doubted.

They arrived back at their table to the waitress delivering fresh drinks, and a message. "From Lana," she said. "Thank you for all you are doing."

"Ohhh," Ali said, looking and finding the singer and her girlfriend sitting at a table along the wall below the dim light of a wall sconce. Ali acknowledged Lana's mouthed "Thank you" with a nod and a smile, and turned to find Dusty smiling proudly at her.

"Well, if you didn't feel appreciated before," she said. "A little Lana Cantrell goes a long way."

"Yes, it does."

"Entertainers like Lana and teachers like Gena have a special appreciation for people who can fight openly for our rights."

Ali nodded. "It's no wonder that Lana comes across from Canada and Gena drives over two hours to get here; it's their safe place. Even a whisper that they're gay and they'd be looking for a different career."

"That's still a lot of trust, don't you think? They don't know who might be here, who might inadvertently say something to the wrong person."

Ali responded with another glance toward Lana's table. "It's a risk they are willing to take. Living in their closet has to be suffocating. It sucks all the air out of life, and leaves no free air to breathe. But there is no life for them outside of that closet."

With a nod, Dusty added, "Everything they do is scrutinized—where they go, who they associate with. They really don't have much of a private life."

"Except here. This place is even more valuable to them than it is to us. At least here they're not in constant fear that the career they had dreamed of will be taken away. They can be themselves and breathe freely."

Dusty coughed and waved her hand to clear the air. "Such as it is."

"Right," Ali replied with a laugh. "It's the best we have. I guess we can't expect it to be perfect."

The DJ's voice broke across the sound system; the lights brightened a shade. "It's that time, ladies, for the last dance of the night. As always, travel safely home as we send you out with the best we can give you—R-E-S-P-E-C-T."

The dance floor filled quickly—last dance, last chance for a while to move freely, express freely, shoulder to shoulder with their community. Their real world.

They sang it together, from the tables to the dance floor. All the voices were joining loudly and strongly in the theme that women everywhere had claimed: R-E-S-P-E-C-T. They were learning what it meant.

The words resonated throughout the bar, women singing them proudly, claiming them and making them their own. Respect. It was what they wanted, needed, and what some weren't afraid to demand.

Dusty held an invisible microphone between them as Ali drove. The words, the music, the rhythm of it carried them home as if they were taking a little of their world with them.

Chapter Seventeen

1989

"The Elliott-Larsen Civil Rights Act 453 of 1976, prohibits discrimination on the basis of 'religion, race,
color, national origin, age, sex, height, weight, familial
status, or marital status' in employment, education,
and access to public accommodations."

Legislative Council, State of Michigan

The courtroom was remarkably unimposing considering the
seriousness of the stakes at hand. It was a room so small that
it only accommodated a table at one end serving as a judge's
bench and two tables end-to-end on each side facing the
center of the room. The number of spectators was limited to
a single row of chairs across the back wall.

Sitting next to her client, Ali studied her opposing counsel
as he offered his opening remarks. Middle-aged and balding,
he presented with old-school confidence what everyone in the
room knew, that there was no binding federal statute that protected against discrimination on the basis of sexual orientation.

"It is up to the individual states," he continued, "to identify
and define what constitutes discrimination and which situ-
ations qualify for protection. Since there is no Michigan

statute that specifically qualifies sexual orientation, school systems can and must be allowed to define and maintain the moral atmosphere for their students." And he droned on about the contract negotiated by the union and the three I's—incompetence, insubordination, immorality—commonly understood as grounds for dismissal. He made the short leap from sexual orientation to immorality and then relinquished the floor.

With a calm professional presence, Ali addressed a court unaccustomed to a woman lead attorney. "Yes," she began, "Title VII, a federal statute that prohibits discrimination on the basis of sex is not binding. What constitutes discrimination is up to each state. And in the Elliott-Larsen Civil Rights Act of 1976, the State of Michigan prohibits discrimination on the basis of 'sex' in employment. In other words, a person's sex cannot be used as the reason for dismissal from employment. And firing a woman who identifies as a lesbian *because* she is a lesbian is sexual discrimination." Ali returned to the table, having stated her case clearly, and keeping it simply focused on inclusion. The decision the court must make was what the word "sex" included.

The superintendent of the school district—sworn in and squaring his shoulders in an air of confidence—had taken the chair next to the judge's table. Attorney George Bennett addressed his client.

"Good afternoon, Mr. Heathe," he began. "For the record, you did terminate Ms. Richardson's employment, is that correct?"

"Yes, her contract was terminated."

"And what was the reason for the termination?"

"She didn't meet the morality clause in her contract."

"The highlighted clause that has been submitted to the court?"

"Yes."

"Would you be more specific, please?"

"Yes. Ms. Richardson is a lesbian," the superintendent replied with a quick glance toward Ali's client.

"And how do you know this?"

"Well, a parent made the allegation, and Ms. Richardson admitted that she was when I asked her about it."

"Thank you," the attorney said with a nod, and returned to his table.

Ali rose, greeted the superintendent, and began her questioning. "What subject did Ms. Richardson teach?"

"I believe it was Freshman English."

"Yes, that's right," she replied. "For the record." She paused for a few seconds, then continued. "Was she a good teacher? Did the students like her, and did she receive good evaluations from the principal?"

"I wasn't aware of complaints from her students or principal."

Ali retrieved papers from her table. "I have copies of Ms. Richardson's last two evaluations, which your counsel and the court also have copies of, both stating that she is an exceptional teacher. I've also submitted copies of a letter written and signed by her students that says things like, 'she makes learning fun, she keeps her classroom open at noon for students who need extra help,' and 'she cares about all of her students.'" Ali made direct eye contact with him. "And yet you terminated her. None of this," she held up the papers, "matters?"

"Well, we're not only responsible for our students' learning, but have to be concerned with the moral environment that we're providing them."

"And what is it that Ms. Richardson has done to affect that atmosphere, to make it unacceptable?"

He looked as if she had asked him if water was wet. Yet he seemed to have difficulty putting together an answer. "Well . . ."

"Didn't you say that you weren't aware of any complaints from students or the principal?"

135

"Yes, but she's still a lesbian."

"Is her being a lesbian apparent in school or in the classroom? Are you aware of her doing or saying anything that would indicate to staff or students that she is a lesbian?"

"No, but . . ."

"You weren't aware of anything, yet you terminated her." Ali motioned dismissively with her hand. "That wasn't a question. Let's say one of your teachers came back to work from lunch, and it was clear that she had had too much to drink. Would that be grounds for termination?"

He stiffened his shoulders and replied, "Sure."

"What if she drank too much with friends in the privacy of her home on the weekend but there was no evidence of it when she came to work on Monday? If you were aware of it, would that be grounds?"

"No, of course not. That's her private life."

"And let's say one of your top women teachers was seen on what looked like a romantic date with a man while her husband was out of town. Would that be grounds for her termination?"

"Not as long as it didn't affect her teaching. That's her private life."

"So why would something occurring in Ms. Richardson's private life be grounds for *her* termination?"

The superintendent stared at her. Wasn't it clear, he must be thinking. "She's a lesbian," he said, as if it really *should* be clear to everyone.

She wanted to shake her head and throw her arms in the air, but Ali maintained her composure. "Then I'm confused, Mr. Heathe," she began. "Are you saying that it's morally right for a woman to cheat on her husband?"

"No, of course not."

"So you can overlook something you consider morally unacceptable as long as it doesn't affect someone's teaching, but not in the case of Ms. Richardson?"

"Well, uh." The comparison was clearly unnerving to him. He repositioned himself in his chair and leaned forward. "You know, whatever goes on between a man and a woman is within what society considers normal. Homosexuality is not. We don't have any guarantee that she won't say or do things that indicate to the students that she is a lesbian and that they should see it as normal."

"So, you have terminated Ms. Richardson's contract based on something that hasn't happened." She waved her hand again. "That wasn't a question. I have no further questions for Mr. Heathe."

"Mr. Bennett," the judge said, "do *you* have any further questions for Mr. Heathe?"

"No, judge."

"Ms. Richardson," the judge addressed.

Ali leaned close to her client and said, "Just be you."

Carrie Richardson nodded and offered a nervous smile. Blond shoulder-length hair tucked behind her ear, she presented well in a waist-length jacket and skirt. She was fresh-faced and young and Ali believed an excellent representation of the professional lesbian. If they had an edge at all, Carrie was it.

"Good afternoon, Ms. Richardson," George Bennett began. "I'm curious …" He hesitated as if he was having second thoughts, but continued. "Why didn't you deny that you're a lesbian?"

Carrie maintained eye contact. "I didn't think that it should matter."

That much Ali knew about her client. She absolutely believed that her sexuality should not matter. But beyond that, she was young enough, hopeful enough to think that it *wouldn't* matter. This was the voice, the presence, whether it was successful now or not, that would make the old guard pay attention. Her simple answer had made a white-haired, over-seventy judge, measure, maybe even reconsider, established thought.

137

Opposing counsel's remaining questions and Carrie's answers were inconsequential. His best attempts were to emphasize Carrie's sexuality, which was already established.

"Do you live with another woman?"

"No."

"Do you frequent lesbian bars to find women to date?"

"I occasionally *take* a date to a bar so that we can have a night out, to have a drink and dance."

"How often is occasionally?"

"A couple of nights a month. Most nights I am grading papers."

"Have any of your female students spent time in your apartment?"

"No," she answered firmly.

Analytically, Ali figured that he was searching for a way to make Carrie appear more like a stereotypical lesbian and less like a woman.

Ali's goal was to marry the lesbian Carrie Richardson to the woman so that she was one under the word *sex*.

"What *does* constitute a typical day for you, Ms. Richardson?" Ali asked.

"Oh, well, it begins early. I'm an early riser. I'm up by five-thirty. A cup of coffee, a quick jog with my little Sheltie, a shower and breakfast, and I'm off to work. I like to be at school early and have everything organized before the students come in. Then it's a day of classes, and an open classroom during lunch. After school I run home, let my dog out, then head back to school to sponsor Student Council or school newspaper, depending on the day. In the evening I either pick up something to eat or heat up whatever I cooked on the weekend, take my dog for a jog, and grade papers."

"I'm exhausted just listening to your day," Ali said with a smile. "What is a typical weekend like?"

"Saturday mornings my colleague, Jason Temple, and I tutor junior high school students at the local library. The afternoon is for my niece and nephew. I do something with them, like a movie or whatever they decide, and that gives my sister and brother-in-law some time to themselves. I reserve Saturday night for me if I'm not too tired. Sunday I sleep in and spend a good part of the afternoon with my parents."

"You don't have much personal social time, do you?"

Carrie smiled. "No, not a lot."

"Do you have more of a personal life during the summer?"

"A bit more. But I teach summer school and take grad classes in the summer."

Was it enough? The question began nagging Ali almost immediately. The questions had been asked, the answers given. Back at the table, Ali complimented Carrie on her composure and presentation. Her only worry, her one doubt, was whether she had brought out the best in her client, offered the best argument.

Opposing counsel's closing comments were simple. "This is not a complicated case. Ms. Richardson clearly is a good teacher. She is also a lesbian. Her sexual orientation puts her outside the intent of the protection of the Elliott-Larsen Civil Rights Act." And that was it. Logic broken down to its barest bones. Protection stripped to naked.

Ali rose and faced the judge. "Mr. Bennett and I do agree on one thing," she began. "This is *not* complicated. Superintendent Heathe testified that Ms. Richardson's abilities and effectiveness as a teacher were not in question and had no bearing on her termination. He stated that his reason for terminating her contract was because she is a lesbian, and that being a lesbian negatively affected the moral atmosphere of the school. Yet, there was no testimony of any negative impact other than admitting her sexuality to Mr. Heathe. She lost her job solely because she is a lesbian—a woman who, in her private life, dates another woman. The Elliott-Larsen Civil Rights Act protects women, as included

139

in the word *sex*, against discrimination in employment. It protects Carrie Richardson from being terminated without cause."

The waiting was actually more stressful than the hearing. Three weeks with no decision, too much time filled with doubting and questioning. Had she done enough, asked the right questions, relied too heavily on what was right versus what had been accepted thought? Ali struggled with the haunting sense of loss, and of being able to find something positive from it if that proved to be the case. Her calls to Carrie Richardson attempted to balance hope with honest possibility. It was all she could do—until today.

Ali opened the PO box, and the notice of a registered letter stood alone. Hurriedly she rushed to the counter and signed for the official envelope. Her intent all along had been to open it with Dusty beside her for support. But she successfully fought the urge to tear open the envelope only until she was in the car. She took a deep breath, slipped her key under the flap, and slid it open.

Her eyes scanned quickly over the document and zeroed in on the wording of the decision. "There is compelling argument for protection of a woman and teacher of Carrie Richardson's qualities. Her contributions to the education of our children are recognized. I recommend that Superintendent Heathe and the Candor-Evans school board reconsider her value as an educator and weigh that value against the possibility of any negative effect that her private life may have on her students." Ali closed her eyes and dropped her head back against the headrest. Shallow breaths fought the pounding of her heart. It was all she needed, all she wanted to read. She'd lost. Carrie had lost. The rest of the decision, though important legally, was moot.

"The court recognizes that this decision will serve as a precedent-setting case, and a decision that further defines the intent of The Elliott-Larsen Civil Rights Act to include the protection of all gays and lesbians would also restrict an employer's right to judge on an individual basis the effect on their work environment. The court, therefore, rules in favor of the defendant."

There it was—the worry that had haunted her—signed and delivered in black and white.

She didn't have to say it. Dusty knew the moment Ali tossed the letter on the coffee table and dropped heavily onto the couch. Dusty sat close beside her and slid her arm around Ali's waist. "What was the reason?" Dusty asked.

Ali dropped her head and leaned forward on her forearms. "The *real* reason?" she asked, not expecting an answer. "All lesbians don't look like Carrie."

"So Justice *doesn't* wear a blindfold."

Ali shook her head. "*That* one sure doesn't."

"You did the best you could, honey."

"Did I?" She lifted her head and sank back into the thick cushion of the couch. "The argument seems so simple. We're either included or we're not."

"To not be is blatant discrimination."

"Or just another way to keep us invisible." Ali closed her eyes and exhaled emotional weariness.

"Someday they won't be able to ignore us. We just can't give up."

Ali stared silently at the ceiling.

Dusty knew her well enough to know that she was taking this personally. She had done all her homework, had practiced her argument in front of Dusty, had even studied the judge—white, seventy-six, Harvard Law, from a family steeped in old money and attorneys. Dusty picked up the letter and read the decision. "You know," she said, interrupting Ali's silent stare, "I don't think your argument could have been any better. Do you realize what an accomplishment it is to get the judge to recommend the reconsideration in the first part of the decision?"

Ali smiled for the first time since she came in. "I aimed Carrie Richardson right at him. Right at his old, straight, patriarchal, thrice-divorced self. I wanted to be sure that he kept his eyes on her. As much as it goes against my core lesbian self, I wanted him to see a beautiful woman, an excellent teacher, and then a lesbian. I wanted him to be personally questioning why she shouldn't be teaching."

"And you did that, or he never would have recommended that the school board reconsider her contract." There seemed to be a noticeable relaxation of the worry lines on Ali's face. "What do you think the chance of that happening is?"

Ali lifted her brow. "Maybe if there is enough support and pressure from the students and parents to reinstate her. The letter from the students was pretty impressive."

"*You're* pretty impressive," Dusty said and planted a kiss on Ali's cheek. "I say that we celebrate that possibility."

"Well, since an appeal to this state's very conservative Supreme Court will likely never get heard, we may as well celebrate what we can."

"Come on," Dusty said as she rose. "I'm taking you out, wining and dining you as they say."

Ali pushed herself up from the couch and wrapped Dusty in a warm embrace. "What would I do without you?"

Dusty smiled against Ali's shoulder. "I'm never going to give you a chance to find out."

Chapter Eighteen

A vacation, a four-day, rent-a-cottage-on-a-lake vacation, that's what was needed. A four-day weekend with no work, no phone, and untethered time to relax and talk and love. Dusty mentioned it first, and Ali embraced it as if it would offer more than Thanksgiving, Christmas, and Easter all rolled into one. It was an easy decision.

Dusty got home from work first and began packing their bags. Fun clothes, comfy clothes, and tennis shoes. No restrictions, no responsibilities. Four whole days to themselves. Something they'd needed for some time. The thought of snuggling together every morning for as long as they wanted, making love in the afternoon, and being wrapped in Ali's arms as the night air cooled and the embers of the campfire died filled her with warmth.

She checked her watch. Ali should be home in about half an hour. Dusty placed the packed bags at the door and sat on the couch with pad and pencil to make a list of groceries to pick up on the way to the lake. All Ali would have to do was shower and change and they'd be on their way.

The phone on the end table rang. The answering machine showed the Dodds and Drake office number, but it wasn't Ali on the other end. "Dusty, this is Emily," said the familiar but somewhat shaky voice of Ali's secretary.

"Yes, Emily. Is everything okay?"

"No, it—it isn't. Ali collapsed, and an ambulance is taking her to U of M emergency."

It felt as if she had been hit in the chest with a boulder. She tried to stand too quickly, and her legs nearly failed her. "I'm going now," Dusty managed and hung up the phone. She took deep breaths, trying to calm the fear. "She's okay," she said, lifting the keys from the hook in the hall. "Just exhausted. Just needs this vacation, that's all."

Dusty gripped the steering wheel hard. Fighting anxious thoughts and rush hour traffic, she rode the bumper ahead of her and squeezed through light after light. Stopped at a light a block away from the emergency lot, she gripped and ungripped the wheel, tried to change her thoughts, to slow her heartbeat. Her only relief was moving again, closing the distance, finally entering the lot. She found the first open space, jumped from the car and raced through the sliding doors of the emergency entrance.

"Can you tell me if Ali Nichols is okay?" She breathlessly asked the woman at the desk. "She was brought in by ambulance just a little bit ago."

The woman scanned a line of clipboards behind the desk. "Are you family?" she asked.

"A good friend," Dusty replied.

"I'm sorry," she said, "I can't give you any information."

"Please," Dusty pleaded, "I just need to know if she's okay."

"You can take a seat and wait for family members if you want."

"But if they don't come? She hasn't seen them in years."

"Just have a seat over there."

Family members. Qualifying only legally, absent from Ali's life for all these years. The woman didn't understand the situation. There wouldn't be family coming to check on her or show their concern, to wish her well soon. No, it wasn't blood family that would do that.

Dusty crossed the hallway to the pay phones, dug change from her pocket and dialed Rory's number. "Please be home," she whispered. "Please."

Just as she was sure that the answering machine would pick up, he answered with a singsong, "Who am I talking to?"

"It's Dusty. I'm at the hospital. Ali collapsed at work, and they won't let me see her or tell me anything."

"U of M?"

"Yes."

"I'm on my way."

Rory arrived only minutes after Emily, Ali's secretary, and her boss. Michael Dobbs, tall and bespectacled, with a sophistication of gray at the temples went straight to the desk. Yet even her boss was denied information.

"Legally only family can see her?" Dusty asked. "Even if they haven't been in her life for over fifteen years?"

"I didn't realize the situation with her family," Michael said, hands in his pockets and a deep frown on his face. "I should have had her make out a power of attorney."

Long agonizing minutes later, as the small group of friends tried to reassure each other, the sliding doors opened again. Dusty grabbed Rory's arm. He followed her focus to a woman with rod-straight posture and white hair heading to the desk, a younger man at her side.

Dusty spoke barely loud enough for Rory to hear. "Her mother and brother." She watched them disappear around the corner, then turned to look directly at Rory. Her eyes were wide, her brow furrowed. "This has to be serious—permission for surgery or something."

Rory nodded. "We'll find out if I have to go all macho on them. We'll find out."

"Maybe as her attorney I can help get some information," Michael offered.

Dusty stepped in closer, tightening the circle of friends and said, "I'm going back there. What's the worse they could do to me?"

"Let me try first," Michael said.

"But I need to be there," she replied—acting as a buffer between Ali and the family that had disowned her, that had seen her only as an embarrassment. Ali shouldn't be facing them alone.

Michael placed a reassuring hand on her arm, then left the group and approached the desk. "I'm Miss Nichols's attorney," he began. "I really need to see her regarding some legal matters."

"I'm sorry," the woman said, then stopped when Ali's mother and brother emerged from the hall. The woman directed her attention to them. "These people are asking about Miss Nichols."

Everyone joined Michael and waited for a response.

Mrs. Nichols looked stoically at each of them and brought her eyes back to Dusty. "You're not family," she said.

"I'm her boss and her attorney," Michael interjected. "We just want to know how she's doing."

Her focus shifted to Michael. "She's not," she said, then added without even a flicker of emotion, "She's gone."

"Gone?" he asked in confusion. "Back home?"

The two of them, standoffish and unresponsive, moved on toward the door. Confusion registered on the faces of the group as they turned to the woman at the desk for an explanation.

Michael continued to take the lead. "Has she been released?" he asked, a logical assumption, an obvious hope.

The woman leaned forward, the lines of her face tightening in anticipation. "No," she said carefully. "Miss Nichols passed away."

The words snatched the air from Dusty's lungs. Her legs weakened and collapsed beneath her. She clenched at Rory's shirt, and he grabbed her arms to hold her up. Her eyes pleaded with his, and her lips tried to form the words but there was no air. Emily helped him lift her to a chair.

Dusty felt the hard plastic of the chair under her and the long, strong muscles of Rory's arms around her. They were real, the only things she was sure of. There was nothing else, only her mind spinning, free-falling into a dark void.

Michael again. "What the hell happened?"

"That's all I know," the woman replied.

He turned abruptly and disappeared down the hall, leaving Emily with her face buried in her hands and Rory trying to console a devastated Dusty.

When he returned, Michael knelt before the grieving friends and said, "Let's go somewhere else."

Rory nodded, wiped the tears from his cheeks and replied, "We can go to my place." He brushed the hair, wet from tears, from Dusty's face. "Come on, honey."

"No," she said, eyes wide, not leaving his, "no, Rory. I can't. I have to see her."

Rory looked at Michael, and Dusty followed his eyes. "No," she repeated, "Not without Ali. Nooo, Rory, I can't."

Rory stood and tried to pull her up with him. "No," she said, wiggling her arms from his grip.

Michael took her hands and said softly, "There are things I need to tell you, Dusty. You need to know, okay?" He looked at Rory. "Emily and I will follow you."

Physically Dusty stopped fighting them. She occupied the passenger seat in Rory's car, made her way from the parking lot to sit in his apartment without her mind leaving Ali. She hadn't spoken, hadn't allowed anything to invade what she held as truth. She heard only the voice that filled her heart, her world. Saw only the face that would never leave her. She held to that truth, held it tightly, protected it against the words that threatened it.

Michael spoke then. The others listened. "She never regained consciousness. They tried everything, but her heart just failed."

Dusty saw the tears making glistening trails down Rory's cheeks. He believed the words. She would not.

The only way that she could keep Rory from saying what she refused to hear was to take the pill he said would let her sleep. He wouldn't let her go home until she slept, so she took the pill. For three days she appeased him. He knew something that she didn't. He knew eventually denial would lose, and the tears would come.

And when they started, it seemed that the tears would never stop. Rory knew that, too, and he knew when to leave her alone to grieve and when to force her to eat, to get up, to take care of herself. It was a process, one Rory knew well.

He'd picked up clothes and essentials for her once he got her settled down, but he had been in no rush to take her back to her apartment. It would just make the process that much longer. Although some days had been better than others, today was not one of them.

Rory's voice sparkled the dull air of the apartment alive the moment he entered. "Eight hours of teenage chatter and angst," he said. "Oh my God, I'm in dire need of sisterhood." He plopped onto the couch where Dusty sat curled around a bed pillow. "Talk to me in beautiful adult gayness."

"I never got to see her," she replied, staring into the void above her. "I never got to say good-bye." She felt tears trickling toward her hairline and wondered where they could be coming from. It didn't seem possible that there could be more tears after so many days and nights filled with them. "Part of me still doesn't believe it's real."

Inches away, Rory dropped his head against the back of the couch and stared into Dusty's void. "It was Marfan syndrome," he began. "My connection at the hospital working on the AIDS project got the information for me. It's genetic.

148

She didn't know she had it." He turned his head and spoke to Dusty's profile. "It causes aorta dilation and weak connective tissue. Her aorta ruptured. There was nothing anyone could have done."

This time she heard the words, accepted the pain of them. She leaned against him and welcomed the gentle embrace. The truth was her world no longer existed. It was gone. Ali was gone, along with reason and purpose and everything that made life worthwhile. They left her that moment as her body crumpled against Rory.

He snugged his arms around her and pressed his lips to the top of her head.

Her words were muffled against him. "I can't keep going without her."

"Shhh."

"I won't. I can't."

"Yes, you can," he whispered against her head.

In the deepest part of her, though, life had hunkered down safely, weathering the worst of her despair. Rory watched her closely, recognizing the stages that he, too, had gone through. It had been easier than he thought to get her excused from work. Dealing with the death of an out-of-state relative brought her an unquestioned two weeks. But the temptation to look for a different job was expected after Dusty lost out for the education program to a new male hire. The decision was on hold for now.

Rory tapped on the bathroom door. "Okay, I took the curlers out of my hair. Let's go to breakfast."

It was the first smile he had seen since she had been there. Dusty emerged from the bathroom with, "How can I say 'no'?"

"I'm irresistible."

"That you are," she replied. "But I think I should go home after breakfast."

149

"Okay," he said, "but I'm going to be honest with you, sister to sister. I don't want you getting to the angry stage alone."

"How many times have you seen me angry?"

He thought for a moment, then shrugged his shoulders. "I don't think I have."

"Then how would you recognize it?"

"It's more important that *you* recognize it."

Normal was gone, that much Dusty accepted. But going home, being where it had all been normal once, was the best she could do. It was all she wanted—to smell the smells, feel the things that had been their life together. For a while she would expect to find her there, to hear her coming through the door, to feel her slide into bed next to her. Just as Rory had expected after David was gone—for a while. But it would fade over time, a new normal taking its place, just as it had for Rory. Rationally she knew. But she needed to feel it for herself.

Rory pulled into the parking lot closest to Dusty's end of the building and parked in an empty space next to Dusty's car. The significance of the space wasn't apparent at first. But as Rory got out of the car he looked at the cars lining the parking lot. "Do you see Ali's car anywhere?"

Dusty looked as well and shook her head. "Didn't you say—"

"Yes, Michael and Emily said that they would bring it back here," Rory said. "I'll call him later. Maybe they left it in the wrong lot."

Rory might have forgotten, but a missing car was deja vu for Dusty. As much as she wanted to believe otherwise, the feeling stayed with her up the stairs to the second-floor apartment and exploded into reality the moment she opened the door.

Two steps in, Dusty stopped abruptly, and Rory nearly

knocked her over. "What the . . ." he said, stepping beside her to see what had stopped her.

The coat closet was open, and jackets lay crumpled on the floor. The living/dining area was stripped of all except the furniture that had come with the apartment. Dusty hurried past the kitchen, its cabinets and drawers open and empty, to the bedroom. It looked like an abandoned apartment that had been ravished by squatters. The bed was stripped, closet door and drawers were open, and clothes were strewn across the floor.

Rory had followed her through. "The door was locked," he said. "I'm talking to management."

He disappeared to get answers, but Dusty knew before he returned. There were no pictures, no personal items, and the clothing left behind was Dusty's. There was nothing left in what used to be their home that acknowledged that Ali had lived there. Dusty moved from room to room, disconnected, searching for reason—something, anything that could snuff out the smoldering anger. But there was no reason, no justified reason, and she had given up. *They* had given up finding the why of it years ago.

And she knew the moment she walked into the bathroom that there was nothing that could stop the anger. She picked up what was left of her toiletries and began throwing them one at a time across the hallway.

Rory dodged a shampoo bottle and called out, "Dusty, it was her family."

Her voice shook with anger. "They took everything," she said, emerging from the bathroom. "They tried to erase her." Her eyes sparked, wide and intense. "As if she was never here, never lived, never loved."

"Well," he replied, "*that's* impossible. *Nobody* can do that. Not even a family as full of ignorance as hers."

Dusty motioned from one room to the other. "Look at this. They took everything that I had left of her."

He placed his hands on her shoulders and turned her to

face him. "No, they didn't. It's not possible. You carry the most enduring parts of Ali with you, in your heart and in your memories, and how you live in this world. What will always be there is her love, her truth, the laughter, and even the tears that only you shared with her. She's part of *you.*"

He wrapped his arms around her and added, "Just as David will always be part of me." He pressed his cheek to the top of her head. "Let's collect what's left of your things. I can't leave you here now."

It surprised her how little she actually owned; so much of what they had shared wasn't hers. And without those things they shared, without the familiar signs of Ali that made this place their home, it just became an arrangement of rooms. Cold, depressingly impersonal, and no longer her home.

They carried what was left of her life there to the car, and Rory took the bag of trash from the kitchen to the dumpster at the end of the lot.

"Dusty," he called before she reached the car. "Dusty, come here. Look."

She hurried to join him as he climbed the side of the dumpster. "What?"

"Look in that box," he said pointing to the box sitting on the ground below him. He looked over the top of the dumpster and added, "I think there's more in here."

Dusty leaned over the box to see a pile of broken glass and picture frames. She began to carefully lift pieces of broken glass but Rory interrupted her. "I'm going in," he said. "Climb up here and tell me what to fish out."

He dropped into the dumpster and Dusty climbed the rungs on the side to peer over the top. "There are books here and reel tapes," he reported.

"Yes," she said, "can you put them in a box?"

He grabbed a couple of intact boxes, filled them, and set them on the top edge of the dumpster.

"Is there a reel-to-reel player?"

Rory waded carefully through garbage bags, paint cans, and broken chairs. "I don't see anything like that." He started to move a bag, and decided to rip it open.

"Oh, no, Rory, you don't have to do that. You're going to be walking through garbage."

"I already smell like a raccoon," he said, ripping open another bag.

Dusty watched as he ripped open bag after bag. "Tell me if anything looks familiar," he said.

"No, nothing," she replied. "Come on, get out of there."

He ripped open two more bags, then made his way to the corner and used a broken chair to scale the side. He lowered the boxes to Dusty and climbed down. "When I saw that first box, I had high hopes of it all being in there. But, you know, they could have been here more than once, and the dumpster could have been emptied once already."

"Thank you for trying."

"It's not just anyone I'd get this stinky for. But there's a hot, soapy shower waiting to make me human again, so let's get these boxes in your car and get home."

Dusty placed the boxes on the floor of what was becoming her bedroom, and started looking through them. The books included those by Gloria Steinem and Bella Abzug, pure feminazi propaganda to the socially challenged. And the tapes they had discarded, predictable if you didn't speak French or had no appreciation beyond champagne music. She sorted through them and lifted the one that quickened her heartbeat and always flooded her senses with the smells and sounds of beginning love—Ali's perfume warmed by her skin, whispered words, and the pureness of Piaf. She held it in her hands and wondered if she would ever be able to listen to The Little Sparrow again. Knowing that it was there was enough for now. She placed it on top of the others and picked up the last box.

It creaked with broken glass as Dusty carefully removed a twisted frame. She turned it over and smiled at the familiar foursome, smiling through the cracks in the glass, clowning that day at the base of Paul Bunyan and his ox. Two of them gone now.

She put it aside and picked up another—Ali introducing Gloria Steinem at the rally at the state capitol. Dusty lifted loose pieces of glass that had protected one of Ali's proudest moments. One of Dusty's proudest moments. She had been so nervous for her, so happy for her.

And the next picture she knew before pulling it from the box. The frame, handmade walnut, picked special. The picture was so close to real that it stopped her breath short. Ali, caught in that moment of intimate honesty—eyes twinkling with affection, the corners of her lips turned in a private sign of love. Dusty opened the back and slid the picture free from the shattered glass. She touched her fingertips to the eyes, the lips, the love she would miss with all of her heart, then held it to her chest and cried.

There was no funeral, no official good-bye so that those who loved and respected Ali could show how much. So a candlelight vigil on the University Diag allowed everyone denied by the family that chance. Hundreds of candles held high lit up the night sky; songs of reverence and remembrance filled the air. Testimonies captured who she was to so many, defined her legacy, and said the words Ali's family would never accept. But that didn't matter now. What mattered was how many lives were brightened and enlightened and empowered by hers. And that their testimonies, their gathering in Ali's honor had shared Dusty's grief.

It surprised her how much sharing that night mattered, how hundreds lifted together prevented the grief from crushing any one of them. Dusty stayed as long as she could, listening and sharing stories even as the crowd was thinning. Finally, the need for quiet thought urged her into "thank yous" and "goodnights," and she wrapped her arm around Rory's waist and they made their way toward the car.

"You're going to be okay," he said with a gentle squeeze of her shoulders. "Like me, you're a lot stronger than you think you are."

Dusty nodded against his shoulder. "Remind me when it doesn't seem worth it."

"Dusty," came a male voice behind them.

They turned to see Michael approaching. "I'm glad I caught you," he said. "Would it be okay for me to stop by for a few minutes tonight?"

"Sure," she replied. "Is everything all right?"

"Yes, I think it is."

They settled at the kitchen table and marveled at the night's vigil over white Zin.

"I'm guessing," Rory offered, "that there were a lot of people there tonight who realized for the first time how many others felt a connection to Ali."

"I'm sure there were," Michael said. "I count myself as one of them. There were so many aspects of her life that I was unaware of."

"So many things she wanted to see changed," Dusty said. "She never stopped trying, no matter how hard the fight. There was so much she wanted to accomplish."

"Her loss was glaringly apparent when I was collecting the files from her desk. I knew how hard she worked, how smart she was, but looking through those files . . ." He looked directly at Dusty. "I've lost what soon would have been my top litigator. Tonight, though, I started to see what so many others have lost." He lowered his eyes from hers. "I can't even imagine," he said and pulled an envelope from an accordion file on the floor. "I put her personal papers in a file here for you. And this, as her attorney," he said, handing her the envelope, "I followed up on for you."

"What is it?" Dusty asked, unfolding official-looking papers.

"A life insurance policy she took out years ago," he replied, "naming you as the beneficiary."

"Why would . . ." Dusty began. Then she nodded. "Years ago—when she was afraid that her father would kill her."

"She wanted to be sure that you were okay," Michael added. "She was limited legally."

Dusty nodded. "Precisely what she was fighting to change."

"You'll need to meet the insurance representative personally so that they can issue a check. I'll go with you if you want."

She nodded again. "Thank you." She stood with Rory, walked Michael to the door, and thanked him again.

Rory turned from the door. "You *didn't* know about it, did you?"

"No, she never said anything. I did always think, though, that she would never back down from her father." She nodded her own confirmation. "I was right."

Chapter Nineteen

2017

Admittedly, the plan was blatantly calculated, but it was the best Dusty could come up with. After all it was her encouragement, her own reemergence from apathy, from powerlessness that had caused the rift. It was, therefore, her responsibility to try to make it right. And Amie's favorite restaurant seemed the perfect place to try.

Amie was right on time and spotted Dusty immediately. "Hi," she said, approaching the booth with a look of concern. "I'm glad you called." She slid into the booth and leaned into direct eye contact. "I've wanted a chance to explain better. It's not that I don't respect, even admire, all that you do to save animals. I do. I want you to know that."

"No, I know you do," Dusty replied. "I'm the one who should explain. So, please let me say what I need to say and then I'll accept whatever you decide to do."

Aimc nodded as the waitress delivered the two cups of coffee Dusty had ordered.

"When I was growing up and finding out who I was, I realized fairly soon that I was on my own. I wanted to go to college, to go into veterinary medicine." She acknowledged the surprised look from Amie. "But others decided that it wasn't appropriate. I wanted to work and live on my own, save money to go back to school—but the only jobs I could get didn't pay enough to do both. And when I fell in love with the most wonderful woman in the world, it almost ruined both our lives. For years we fought hard for the rights that we deserve, that all women deserve, but the ERA never passed. I knew that I was kickin' rocks, that as painful as it was I had to keep kicking. And I did, we did—until I lost Ali. That was a pain too intense. I stopped kicking. I gave up. Until the day I saw a man throw a bag into the river in the park. I waded in and pulled it out. Saving those puppies gave me new purpose. It led to an abandoned dog and then a burned cat, and unadoptables and a mission that finally let me sleep at night. There are a number of organizations and shelters doing what they can, but I have a lot of animals that are here because, as I found out early in life, I couldn't count on anyone else."

Dusty stopped. There had been no expression of dismissal, no sign of indifference. Nothing to indicate judgment or contempt. Amie was just listening, so Dusty continued. "More importantly, I want you to know that taking that dog, ignoring the risk for ourselves and to your relationship, is on me. Jada never would have done that on her own. The dog would have died because none of the organizations or the police that should have wouldn't challenge a big militia mucky-muck. Jada tried all the right channels, and every day the dog got weaker. After the last 'sorry, we can't help you,' I was the one who made the decision. I would have tried it myself but Jada ... Well, Jada was worried that these old legs couldn't outrun the end of a rifle." She offered a less than convincing frown, adding, "She was wrong, but ..."

Amie's smile was subtle, a gentle understanding. "Thank you," she said softly.

Dusty believed the sincerity in Amie's eyes. She wanted to believe that it would be enough for her to give the relationship another chance. They both needed time, Dusty had decided. Time to talk, time to revisit what they loved about each other. She owed them that.

Dusty looked up as everything started to come together and Jada entered the restaurant expecting advice over dinner. When Dusty raised her hand to get her attention, Amie turned to see Jada approaching their booth. The look that Amie shot at Dusty was razor-sharp with suspicion, and it was felt.

"Just—" Dusty began.

"Trust you?" Amie snapped back. "I almost did."

"Look," Dusty said, sliding to the edge of the booth, "this was all me. She didn't know anything about it."

"About what?" Jada asked. "What's going on?"

Dusty stood and offered her seat to Jada. "You need to talk, that's all. Just talk," she said, squeezing Jada's arm. "Please." Before either could respond she turned toward the door and left them alone.

Jada stood silently.

"You didn't know about this?"

Jada made eye contact and shook her head.

After an awkward few seconds, Amie asked, "Are you going to sit down? I really want you to sit down."

"I don't see how talking is going to change anything. It won't change who we are."

"No." Another awkward pause. "But what if it helps us better understand who we are?" She held Jada's eyes and added, "I want that. Don't you?"

Jada slid into the booth. "Yes," she replied. "I didn't think *you* did."

"I didn't until Dusty pulled this stunt. I might not have admitted it to her, but what she told me about herself is making me look at things differently."

"What did she tell you?"

"In a nutshell, she told me who she is," Amie began. "In a few words she told me how an independent-thinking young lesbian had very little control over the direction her life took.

So she learned to take control over whatever she could." Jada listened intently. "I knew that there were constraints on women then that we don't have; it just was never so personal. My mother always seemed content with her life, with her role as a mother and wife. I wasn't privy to the anguish Dusty endured. My mind is racing over all the things in my life that have been my decision, my choice. It makes me wonder about how restrictive my mother's, and now Dusty's, life must have been as a young girl. Did my mother ever want anything different for her life? Dusty did."

"I admit that I was very self-absorbed," Jada said. "Until we rescued Brandy, I never asked Dusty anything about her life, nothing past the animals. Just what I could see. That was it."

Amie nodded. "How much do we even know about each other? What we see? What we feel? I know I love how your brows lift together above your nose when you're about to laugh. I love your compassion—and your passion. But there's so much I don't know."

"I think part of me didn't want you to know too much for fear you wouldn't like what you learned. Can you say I was wrong?"

Wrong? Amie thought. No. She couldn't say that. What she was ready to admit was, "*I* was wrong." Her frown was tight, pensive. "I couldn't see past 'right is right,' 'protocol above all.' I couldn't understand how anyone could. It's confusing to me—messy—outside the clear, clean lines I'm used to. I'm sorry," she said, moving her coffee cup aside and reaching across the table to take Jada's hand. "I have no right to judge your heart."

Jada squeezed Amie's hand. "I never expected to step beyond the boundaries or disregard the rules, not consciously. I just found that if there was a way to save a life I was willing to go there. I never intended to compromise our relationship. I am so sorry." She looked down at their hands for a moment, then looked up and added, "I can only promise that I will never knowingly do that to you again. But what I can't promise is that I won't step past the line again. I learned how much I needed to do whatever was necessary and how much anguish I felt when I thought there was nothing more I could do. I broke down in front of Dusty and cried when I knew that dog was going to die without help." She hesitated, and the realization centered itself. "It didn't change who I am, it made me realize *exactly* who I am. I am stronger than I thought I was. More valuable than I thought I was. More compassionate, more committed. I've learned a lot about myself."

Amie released Jada's hand, leaned close over the table and caressed the side of Jada's face. "And I've learned how much I love you." She held the gaze that she had missed over the past weeks, let her fingers linger against Jada's cheek, and didn't notice the waitress approach their booth.

"Excuse me," the woman said.

"Oh, I'm sorry, Jackie," Amie replied, looking up. "Yes, are you up for some comfort food?" she asked Jada.

But the waitress interjected quickly. "No, I'm not here to take your order, doctor. I have to ask you to leave."

Amie's blank expression changed quickly into one of confusion. "What?" she replied.

"I've been told to ask you to leave."

"Why?"

"There's been a complaint."

"By whom? Is Eileen here? Is the owner here?"

"Yes."

"Please tell her that I'd like to talk with her."

As the waitress left for the back of the restaurant, Jada asked, "What is going on? Are we taking up a booth too long without ordering?"

"I don't see anyone waiting for a table. She hasn't worked here long. I'll talk with Eileen and get it straightened out."

There was no mistaking owner Eileen Bingham— professionally coiffed and stylishly dressed in skirt and heels.

161

She approached without hesitancy and with a greeting far too formal for the amount of time she had known Amie. "Dr. Luca."

"Eileen, hi. How's the new grandbaby? I haven't had a chance to—"

"She's fine," was Eileen's noticeably terse response.

"Oh, good," Amie said, noticing the unusually rigid hold of her head and the tight lines of her mouth. "I'm sorry if we were taking up a booth too long. We absolutely intend to order some of your best comfort food."

"I'm sorry, doctor," Eileen replied, her eyes making only fleeting contact. "You and your friend need to leave."

"Eileen, what's all this about? How long have I been coming here?"

"This is a family restaurant. Your *behavior* is making other customers uncomfortable."

Anger had replaced Jada's initial surprise. "Holding someone's hand, touching her face? If that makes someone uncomfortable, then that's *their* problem, not ours."

The confrontation had drawn the attention of others around them. A man from the booth behind them stood and addressed Eileen. "Is there a problem? Do you need some help?"

Jada slid to the edge of the booth and stood directly between the man and Eileen. "There's no problem," she said, holding her hand out to Amie.

Hand in hand they left the restaurant without another word. Once in the parking lot, Amie's agitation was evident. She broke contact with Jada and walked ahead at a gait more suited for chasing snakes. Focusing somewhere over the roofs of the parked cars, she'd start in one direction and then abruptly change to another.

Jada followed a few steps behind until Amie turned to face her. "What is happening, Jada?" she asked, arms flaying at her sides. "Do you realize how long I've been coming here?"

"I want to know if one retro-minded customer is all it took to kick us out."

Amie's focus wandered across the dusk-softened space over the parking lot. "You know," she began, "My parents have worried. I've had friends and people who wondered and questioned." Her focus finally centered on Jada. "But I have never been humiliated like this."

"And I've never been this angry," Jada added. "But I think we know someone who has." Jada pointed to her car. "Come on. We'll pick your car up after."

"Yep," Dusty directed at her two shaken guests, "it's like a samurai sword took you down at the knees. Your foundation is gone."

Both Amie and Jada nodded. "You've been there, haven't you?" Jada asked.

"Oh, too many times to count."

"So what did you do?" Amie asked. "What do *we* do?"

Dusty rested her forearms on the old oak kitchen table and looked across at the familiar mix of emotions on her friends' faces. "You got a couple of hours to give me?"

Jada looked to Amie for her answer. "I've got as long as you're willing to put up with us."

"You know I'll camp out here if I have to," Jada added.

Dusty offered her most empathetic look, as soft a look as they would get tonight. "Look, I know that this shook you up. It would most people whether they admitted it or not. You've both come of age in a," she raised her eyebrows, "more comfortable time."

"I don't think either of us doubt that," Amie offered.

"Then with that in mind, the first thing I'm going to tell you is that I won't listen to any whining or crying about this, or anything else that happens. That may sound harsh, but believe me it gets you nowhere."

"So what did you do?" Amie asked.

"After we whined? It depended on who we were dealing with. Sometimes you can do something right away; sometimes you have to see the bigger picture and map a strategy. And you have to decide if the risks are too high and you can't live with them. There were times when I wasn't sure." Looking into the faces of these two young women caused an emotional stirring that she couldn't avoid. Old feelings, old emotions were brought back by the innocence and uncertainty staring back at her. She'd left all that behind— experienced it, conquered it at times, and moved finally to a place of costly peace. But here she was, after so many years, letting the energy of it invade that peace.

"In the sixties and early seventies," she began, "my Ali was a rising star in the feminist movement." The vision of her, even after so much time, was as vivid as today's sunrise. Dusty's focus rested vaguely on the center of the table. "A shining star with all the attributes that the movement loved and needed—beautiful, charismatic, and as smart as they come. She drew large crowds on campuses and got the attention of the big names in the movement. But the more attention and publicity she got, the more embarrassing she became to her father—not someone you want to embarrass. He was an old school 'women in their place' police detective. It was easy for him to have his police buddies harass the hell out of her, and me when he realized who I was to her. But when she continued to be a public embarrassment, he stepped up his game."

Just the memory of Ali, standing proudly before a large group of women, speaking the truth of their lives and their hopes, brought with it a wave of nostalgic pride. And it sounded in her voice. "One rally on campus had been advertised all over for a couple of weeks. Ali Nichols was leading the rally. It must have infuriated her father because she hadn't spoken more than ten minutes before the police arrived. There was no warning, no request to disperse, just an arrest and an order for the women to go home and cook dinner. The officers handled Ali as if they were containing a dangerous murderer. Our heroine was taken down right before our eyes, and the point was made. The cuffs were so tight she had bruises for weeks."

"What was she arrested for?" Jada asked.

"Oh, disturbing the peace, of course. Disturbing the peaceful status quo of *their* women."

Amie seemed stunned. "Her own father?"

Dusty nodded. "No surprise to either of us. A lot of us protested, got arrested, paid our fines. It became a pattern. It was expected. We knew what to do. But months later something happened that Ali and I were not prepared for. It was as if Ali had stepped on a rake; it came out of nowhere." She paused for a moment. The memory of the look of hurt on Ali's face still clutched her heart.

But Jada was impatient. "So what happened?"

"Ali had proven herself. She was talented enough, strong enough, charismatic enough to be elevated statewide to giving the warm-up speeches and introducing the major speakers like Gloria Steinem and Bella Abzug. She was so excited, and our life together was so exciting. We lived together, organized together, and we were making history. Michigan ratified. Then the rake. Phyllis Schlafly was doing her best all over the country to build resistance to ratifying the ERA. And one of her shivs was the danger of normalizing homosexuality, and that the movement was filled with lesbians. A number of states had ratified, but her message was scoring points and thirty-eight states were needed to ratify before the deadline. So decisions to mitigate damages were being made from high up in the movement. Right after a huge regional rally one of the main organizers took Ali aside. The question was to the point and direct, 'Are you a lesbian?' Ali's answer was just as direct: 'yes.' It certainly hadn't escaped them that wherever Ali was, I was

165

there. The implication was clear. So, despite her talent and dedication, she was told that they could no longer use her in the movement."

"God," Amie declared. "She must have been devastated."

Dusty nodded. "Way beyond what I had expected from her father's betrayal. She was such a strong woman, but this dropped her to her knees. I was heartbroken for her."

"How did you get through it?" Jada asked.

"First, in the middle of a tear-filled night, I told her that I wanted her to go ahead without me. It was the hardest thing I had ever said."

Amie reached for Jada's hand and held it tightly.

Over forty years later, Dusty still fought tears, eyes glistening. "I don't know, even now, how I would have made it through if she had agreed. But she didn't. We held each other as if it were our last night together, and in the morning, she said, 'Promise me one thing. Wherever we go, whatever we do, we do it together.' It was a promise we never broke."

"Thank you," Amie said, wiping her own watery eyes. "You've certainly put this whole thing in perspective."

"You won't have to worry about me whining," Jada interjected. "I'm angry at what happened to Amie, and I would have been furious at what happened to Ali."

"We *were* angry," Dusty replied. "Hurt has a way of evolving into anger, and anger evolving into resolve. We finally got to resolve. We and other identifiable lesbians were expendable for the greater good: to get the ERA passed for all women and then work for our rights later."

"But it *didn't* pass," Jadded added. "Maybe a lot of talented, dedicated lesbians could have made a difference."

Dusty shook her head. "Probably not, but we'll never know. It taught us, though, that we needed to be in for the long haul—to make connections, to keep organizing from the grass roots up, and to keep educating."

"Kickin' rocks?" Amie asked.

"Sometimes you can get enough people kickin' a rock that they'll actually move the damn thing. Look what happened with marriage equality."

Amie turned to Jada, held her attention for a moment, then asked Dusty, "So what do we do?"

"For right now, kick the rock you can move," she replied. "There's someone I have to talk to and then we'll talk again tomorrow."

Chapter Twenty

Exhilarated, was that the right word? Dusty showered and dressed earlier and quicker than usual, thoughts and ideas jumping from one to another faster than she could grab them. What would have the biggest impact? Who should be involved? What would spark a fire but not burn down the building? Dusty slipped into her boots, took no time to tie the laces and hustled out to the barn and her favorite coconspirator.

The opening of the barn's side door startled Rory. "Oh, Holy Mary!" he exclaimed, splaying a bony hand against his chest. "Don't frighten a girl like that. She'll soil her whities."

Dusty laughed. "I'm sorry, honey."

"What are you doing out here so early?"

"We need a plan."

"We who?" He poured a scoop of dry food into one of a dozen stainless steel bowls, and continued filling bowls while Dusty filled in the reason for her unusual agitation.

"So," she said as he stood and faced her, "we need a plan."

Rory crossed his arms and tilted his head. "Well, *there* you are," he said, "all dusted off and decked out in full armor. It suits you so much better," he added with a sly grin.

Dusty flung her arms out from her sides and matched the tilt of his head. "Decked out for action, and—"

"And it's a damn good thing your best girlfriend has kept

her place in the community. Come on, let's get everyone fed and then set up a war room in the kitchen. A few well-placed phone calls and we will be in business. *You*," he said, "need to find out what the busiest night is for the restaurant."

The parking lot began to fill before the dinner rush. Per the plan, Jada and Amie waited in the car until they saw Dusty pull in. Following her were two large motorcycles with two riders each.

"Are you ready for this?" Jada asked.

"I'm not sure how a bunch of people doing a sit-in is going to make any impact."

"Me either, but Dusty is signaling us to join her."

"Okay," Amie replied, opening the car door, "here we go."

As they approached Dusty's car, the motorcyclists, minus their helmets, joined them. "Your Dykes on Bikes checking in," said a large woman in jeans and leather jacket. Her riding partner in a leather vest and shoulder-length salt and pepper hair hugged Dusty and added, "It's been so long, we thought we'd lost you forever."

"She's like an old bear coming out of hibernation," came a male voice from the other side of the car.

Jada turned as a facsimile of an aging movie star in a blond wig and tight blue dress nearly tripped rounding the back of the car. "This old queen," he mumbled, "hasn't strapped these heels on in years."

Jada smiled. "Rory?"

"In all her glory," he replied. "Trying not to fall on her skinny ass."

"Okay," Amie declared, "I get it now. God, Eileen is going to have a stroke."

"Oh, you haven't seen anything yet," Dusty added. "Let's get going. We go in first," she directed at Jada and Amie.

"Five-minute intervals?" Rory asked.

"Right."

The three of them, dressed in normal everyday attire, seated themselves without incident, ordered drinks, and began examining the menu.

"Is everyone going to order?" Jada asked.

"You bet," Dusty replied. "We're going to make it hard for management to kick out just one or two, and if they try to clear the place, it's going to be costly."

Dusty surveyed the four other occupied tables as the first biker couple entered and chose a table. One man stared, but most paid no attention.

The waitress had taken their orders by the time the second biker couple chose a booth on the other side of the restaurant. They garnered passing glances. Waitresses in different sections were taking customer orders—nothing overwhelming—a plan working just as anticipated.

A family of four came in just ahead of Justin and his new boyfriend, one of the few couples in Rory's large circle who exemplified the gay stereotype—Justin slight and effeminate, and Dan buff and masculine. The family started to seat themselves in a booth, but when Justin and Dan chose the booth next to them, they moved to another.

And then came the big guns.

There was already a bit of a private buzz between two of the waitresses, but they continued to take orders and serve their tables. Dusty watched closely between bites as more regular customers began showing up. Things were about to change.

First came James, full makeup and a summer dress, convincingly beautiful until his voice betrayed him. And behind him, Darian, longtime entertainer, popular because he actually sang Liza Minnelli's songs instead of lip-synching them. His resemblance, together with signature short skirt ensemble, tipped the scale. There was no doubt of an invasion now, which brought the hostess hustling to the front of the restaurant.

She took her place just in time to meet Jerry Gordon,

First One Bank's loan counselor, in full drag. He smiled at the hostess and said, "Oh, Janice, I'm so much later than usual. I'm surprised that my regular booth is open." He breezed by her as she struggled for recognition until she saw him ease into the booth next to the counter. "My usual Earl Grey, Wendy," he said to a confused waitress. "Thank you."

A now aware Eileen made her way from the back of the restaurant. Halfway there an older man stood and followed her to the front. He leaned in close between Eileen and the hostess. "What are you turning this into?"

"I'm not turn—"

But the hostess grabbed her arm as a smug Rory walked in. "What are your specials tonight?" he asked.

"Well," Dusty said, with delight registering on her face, "we've still got it!"

Both Jada and Amie continued to scan the room in awe. The timing had been perfect, the execution flawless. As they watched the reactions, the plan was about to impact. It was like watching the inner workings of a machine as each part clicked into place to move the next.

Eileen seemed paralyzed while her hostess rotely recited the specials. The older man had not left Eileen's side and persisted as Rory took a seat in Jerry's booth. "What are you going to do about this?" he asked.

The hostess stood ready for some kind of directive. Eileen looked as if she was playing the "Freeze" game—statue-like, her eyes frozen in a stare. But no one else was playing. The man, more animated now, asked for some action while the plan shifted into full gear.

"What do you think she is going to do?" Jada asked.

"I don't know," Dusty replied. "But she's going to have to decide. Look around."

The signal had been Rory joining Jerry's booth. Once he was settled and had ordered something to drink, the shift was on. Each couple began by holding hands across the table, allowing time for others to notice and those with issues to react. Then the ante went up. One of each of the couples reached across the table and touched the other's face—a caress or a rearranging of a lock of hair and settling into a gentle hold.

At first there were only stares and whispers here and there, but it only took one customer to move push to shove. The older man had left Eileen's side, returned to his table, and retrieved his wife. His movements, as if saving his wife from a burning building, now had the attention of even those who had ignored the plan playing around them. They watched as he led his wife by the hand to confront Eileen once again.

Eileen had snapped out of her trance and assessed the situation. The plan was obvious and now the man was in her face, nearly nose to nose, demanding that she do something. Most dinners were interrupted and conversations halted—the air in the room stilled. A number of cell phones were recording, and all eyes were on Eileen. Dusty, Jada, and Amie were mesmerized. It was decision time. Could she demand that all *offending* persons leave? Make an example of just a few? Would it even be legal? And if she comped their meals and asked the disturbed couple to leave, would others follow, and would it damage her business?

She took a step back, used her hands to protect the space between them and to offer calm. It was that move and the look of complete loss that made Amie wince—a feeling she hadn't expected. She tried to see herself in Eileen's place but couldn't.

It wasn't clear what Eileen's decision was, if she had in fact made one. But it became irrelevant when two police officers entered the restaurant. With all the cell phones it was inevitable that someone would call them.

There was some sorting out to begin with, and listening. Who was the owner? What was the problem? Both officers looked around the room, getting a sense of what could have caused the disturbance. That quick scan told them all they needed to know. With a look of affirmation from one officer to the other, the older officer addressed the man and his wife. "Okay," he said, "I understand that when you're faced with things that you're not used to it can make you uncomfortable."

"It's not normal," the man returned. "It's disgusting. How are we supposed to enjoy our dinner?"

"So what are you asking Mrs. Bingham here to do?"

"Well," he said, stiffening his back and looking directly at Eileen, "get 'em the hell outta here."

"Okay," the officer replied, "here's the problem Mrs. Bingham has with that. She has a business that serves the public, and those people haven't done anything illegal."

The man seemed unsure, as if waiting for some sort of clarification or choice of options. His wife, though, understood. She took his arm and said, "Come on, Carl, let's just go."

But he stood his ground and ignored her.

The second officer made it clear. "It won't make any difference whether Mrs. Bingham agrees with you or not, and I'm not going to ask her. She can't just kick people out of her business when they haven't done anything wrong."

"It *is* wrong," the man persisted. "Nobody should have to see that."

"Sir," the older officer said, "you need to sit down and finish your dinner without further disturbance, or you need to leave the restaurant."

"Whatever you decide," said Eileen, "your meals are on the house."

The decision was quick. His options were clear. Carl took his wife's hand and started for the door, adding a parting shot. "And we won't be back."

Before they could get out the door, another couple left

their table and followed them. "We won't either," the man added, squeezing past Eileen and the officers. "We'll give our business to a family-friendly place."

Eileen seemed afraid to look around, to see if her nightmare was about to come true. But Dusty watched closely, noticing indecision in the family of four with dad on the edge of his seat, and others watching and waiting to see if it would be a mass exodus. But when no one else got up, it seemed as if the rest took a deep breath and relaxed.

The officers saw it as their cue to wind things up. They left a card in case of further problems and turned toward the door. The applause started with a man sitting with his teenage son and daughter behind the bikers and spread rapidly throughout the restaurant. Rory caught Dusty's eye and tilted his head, shrugged his shoulders, and smiled as though he had just eaten the canary. Eileen, on her way to the counter, stopped abruptly, changed course and headed for the back of the restaurant. She made no eye contact, offered no change of expression, only continuing on and letting the applause die out behind her.

"Do I look stunned?" Amie asked.

Dusty smiled, gave a nod across the room to Rory, and replied, "You look like a new generation beginning to realize its power."

Jada leaned into the conversation. "So we had the law on our side all along?"

"You did, because The Freedom of Religion Act didn't pass here. But that doesn't mean that sometimes you won't have to claim your rights. *Knowing* them is only part of it. Sometimes you may have to decide whether that right is worth fighting for, whether you are willing to risk the consequences. If it's worth it to you, then you plan your battle."

"I never thought I'd have to make those decisions," Amie said. "Participating in the Women's March made me feel part of a bigger movement. I absorbed the energy and the power of it. It took away some of my fear. But *this* battle," she turned to look at Jada and took her hand, "was so personal. I felt singled out and alone . . . and responsible for putting Jada through it."

Jada shook her head. "It just made me mad, and frustrated because I didn't know what to do. I felt awful walking out like we were criminals, but I was too uncomfortable to make an even bigger scene."

"It *is* uncomfortable," Dusty added, "making a scene, resisting, especially when you feel alone. But there are two things that you need to know. You will have to get comfortable being uncomfortable—and you're not alone."

Chapter Twenty-One

Amie met Dusty at the front desk, short-circuiting the hospital's check-in procedure. "Come on back, Dusty. Your Brandy will be excited to see you."

"Oh, I'm glad to hear that," she replied, following the doctor down the hall to a room of kennels. "Thank you, Amie. I seem to be getting a prerecorded answer to every inquiry."

"Yes, you should have called my cell earlier." One whine out-sounded the others as Amie approached Brandy's kennel on the floor level. "Oh, look at this pretty girl," she said, opening the kennel door for a wiggling, whining Brandy.

"Yes, she is a pretty girl," Dusty added as she bent down to fuss over a much-improved dog. "Two weeks ago, I didn't give her much of a chance. I knew we had to try, though."

"She's a fighter. Wagging her tail the whole time anyone was near, even when she could barely lift her head. She just grabbed everyone's heart. Josh sat with her every night before he left and sang to her," Amie said.

The very dry, sparse brandy-colored coat now had a bit of a sheen, and a few pounds of added weight were beginning to cover protruding bones.

"So, give me some real answers, Amie. Is she well enough for me to take it from here?"

"Oh, believe me, if you can take over Rudy's physical therapy and bring her through like you did, Brandy will be easy-peasy."

"That's great news. It's just gotten so expensive, and it didn't sound like Dr. Thayer would release her yet. If it's for necessary care that I can't give that's one thing, but if I can do it myself, you know I will."

"Well, he's on vacation for the next couple of days, so I'm releasing her today. I'll send the food and vitamins with you, and the medications and directions. Once she's full weight and healthy we'll set up an appointment to spay her."

Dusty knelt and accepted grateful kisses from her new boarder. "We'll take good care of you, girl—good food, new friends, and lots of love."

"I just want you to know, Dusty, that I am really glad that you rescued her. I admit the first day I saw her and realized how much she thrived on our attention, how hard she fought to live, that I understood what Jada saw each day. There are some animals whose souls are so magnetic that they draw you in immediately and won't let you go. Brandy is one of those."

Dusty nodded, pulled a collar from her pocket, and placed it around Brandy's neck as she wiggled forward on her forelegs. "Just like some people."

Amie waited to make eye contact and nodded. "Yes, just like some people."

Dusty walked Brandy to the front desk to check out and faced a questioning staff. "Did Dr. Thayer release her?" The office manager asked.

"No," Dusty replied. "Dr. Luca did. She is bringing the food and medications and the bill up in a few minutes."

"I didn't think this dog was ready to be released." The manager had turned to another staff member and lowered her voice. Her expression, though, said enough. She was not pleased with the decision, and she was not pleased with

Amie. For a moment Dusty was tempted to let them keep Brandy longer for Amie's sake.

Amie's confident air, though, quelled the temptation. She placed a bag on the counter and handed Brandy's file to the desk staff. "Written directions for the medication are in the bag," she told Dusty. "And there's a chart for you to keep track of her weight. Call me if you have any questions," Amie said and followed with a bright smile.

She waited while Dusty put the admittedly large charge on her credit card, then walked her to the door. "Call my cell, Dusty, if you have any questions. Things should be fine, though."

Dusty kept her voice low. "Are you sure this is going to be okay? The manager is not a happy woman."

"She rarely is. Don't worry."

A look back at the desk, though, did make Dusty worry. The woman that handled the file had her head down in paperwork. The manager was seriously deep in a phone conversation. "The whole vibe I'm getting, though, doesn't feel right. I don't want to be the cause of putting you in the hot seat."

"Look, if I end up in a hot seat it will be because I did the right thing, and no other reason," Amie said with a hand on Dusty's arm. "You get Brandy home and comfortable, okay?"

"I will. Thank you, Amie."

Amie didn't need Dusty to point out the barely concealed disapproval. There were days, like today, when the sense of it was almost tangible. And lately, she could predict it. The day she spent extra time to calm a woman before her cat was to have major surgery, or when it was noticed that she didn't charge someone for a sample medication that was free to the hospital, and the day she gave out a recipe for a healthy alternative to the special manufactured food that the hospital carried. All had been standard practice under the former owners. They were good practices that fostered trust and appreciation, and had endeared Amie and her original coworkers to people who had counted on this hospital for years. And to think that this wouldn't be a big part of this afternoon's staff meeting would have been a wish too far.

Office Manager Gena Watkins was a female version of what Amie's father would have called a company man. Fully vested, committed to her rise in the corporation, she reasoned in corporate talk, and addressed the staff, as she usually did, with protocol—two positives and a negative.

"For those of you who have been champing at the bit to be able to enter everything electronically, you can begin doing that tomorrow morning. Case by case information entered in real time will go directly to the main computer and save having the staff enter it manually."

Nods from table to table counted the news as a positive and Amie checked off good news number one in her head and waited for number two.

"Now some of you have asked about offering pet insurance," Gena Watkins continued, handing out trifolded pamphlets. "This information will be made available for customers at the front desk, and you can now include a pamphlet after each appointment."

Can include. The growing cynic that had crept into Amie's thoughts lately interpreted that to mean "must include." She wondered how beneficial the insurance would actually be. Amie looked through the information quickly and promised herself to investigate it before encouraging anyone to purchase it.

"Now for those who are still having difficulty adjusting to the changes in practices," she made sure to make eye contact with Amie, Ted Markum, and Ernie Smith, all sitting at the same table. "Seven months is more than adequate time to make those adjustments. Noncompliance will no longer be met with minor disciplinary action. Disregard for company policy will be grounds for dismissal."

Ted leaned over and spoke quietly. "Think she wants to get rid of us?"

Amie raised her hand to get the manager's attention. "Can I ask a question?"

"Yes, what is it?"

"Some of the changes in policy I understand. I may not agree with them, but I can see why they might have been made. But I don't understand such strict limitation on time. Sometimes it's important to take the time necessary to reassure or to explain and answer questions, or to quell fears. There really is no way to anticipate how much time will be needed. It's not something that fits neatly into a time slot."

"I realize that it's easy to lose track of the fact that this is a business," Gena Watkins replied, "but it is. And time *is* money. If you feel it is necessary to spend extra time, then do it with a phone call after hours."

Her tersely clipped sentence deterred Amie from arguing that there were times when that wasn't feasible. A disapproving frown was all she offered in return. She had opened the door, though, as Ted quickly stepped up.

"I have something that I am very concerned about." He continued without giving manager Watkins a chance to close the meeting. "The last surgery I did was originally planned to include a minor second procedure while the animal was under sedation. You canceled the second procedure and rescheduled it for a later date. Not only is that a lot of unnecessary cost for the customer, but it is also added risk to the animal, especially older animals."

"The corporate policy is in place to avoid putting the animal at risk for being under for too long." Another terse reply, but Ted wasn't about to accept the rationale.

"Those types of procedures don't require any additional

time under. The animal would be under anesthesia for the same length of time regardless. These decisions should be left to the doctors who best know the animal and the health situation. This policy serves only to pad the bill."

The look on Gena Watkins' face, tight and stern, left no doubt that the meeting was over. She made sure to douse the chance of further challenges to policy. "I am here to answer your questions, not to challenge corporate policy. Have a nice weekend."

The three of them remained seated at the table as the room emptied. No one spoke until everyone else was gone. Ernie broke the silence. "Well," he began, after clearing his throat, "my wife has been trying to get me to retire for a year now. I think I just made my decision."

Amie shook her head. "I know I'm being selfish, but I wish you wouldn't."

"Count me selfish, too," Ted added. "We count on your wisdom, Ernie. I think we have a smart, talented team here, and Amie and I both value that the three of us can consult together. You'd be breaking up a hell of a team."

"I wouldn't be seriously considering it," Ernie replied, "and I don't think Marie would be so persistent if my professionalism wasn't being compromised."

Amie looked at Ted. "You and I may have only two options if we stand by our convictions," she said. "We can quit or wait to be fired."

Chapter Twenty-Two

Whether they were unwilling or merely procrastinating, neither Amie nor Ted Markum had decided to quit. Two weeks later, though, a decision was unavoidable. The inevitability had hung over every day, every decision in those past weeks. Today Amie pushed knowingly past the edge.

Amie looked into the concerned eyes of seventy-five-year-old Ella McCormick and lifted her little thirteen-year-old terrier mix from the examination table. "The biopsy was benign," she explained of the growth next to the dog's left eye. "But since we have to take care of the abscessed molar, I would prefer to remove the growth while we have her under. This growth is just going to get bigger and eventually push against her eye and make it more difficult to take off. And at her age I really don't want to put her under again if we don't have to."

Ella nodded, but the concern had not left her eyes. "I wish you didn't have to put her under at all."

"I know you worry," Amie said, stroking the little dog's head, "but we have to take care of that infection. We'll give her only what's necessary. We'll take very good care of her."

Another nod from Ella. "I know you will," she said, placing her hand over Amie's. "You know she's my best friend. I don't know what I would do without her."

"She's going to be just fine. You try not to worry. I will give you a call when we're out of surgery."

"My neighbor and I will do some grocery shopping and then go to lunch. She's a good friend and wants to keep me busy so I won't worry so much."

Ella kissed her little dog on the head. "Yes," she said, "I love my little girl." Then she looked at Amie. "Can I take her home today?"

"I think that will be fine. As soon as she is alert and not too wobbly to go to the bathroom outside I'll give you a call."

The surgery went smoothly, and Amie's call relieved Ella's concern. But Amie's concern hung over her throughout the day. Ted caught her in the back hall.

"Anything yet?" he asked, aware that Amie had made the decision to do both procedures that morning.

"No, but the step too far is going to be my releasing the dog to her owner today and not keeping her overnight. I'm probably writing my own pink slip. The owner is on her way."

"Ernie already left for home, but you've got me for backup."

Amie tilted her head and smiled. "You're a fine doctor and friend, Ted. And I am not going to be responsible for your pink slip."

"You won't be."

She left him in the hall and retrieved Ella's little dog from her kennel. Amie carried her—alert, wrapped in a blanket, and sporting a soft cone—to a front examination room. Minutes later Ella McCormick met her with a smile that erased any thought of pink slips.

Amie handed the anxious bundle to Ella and explained, "She came through everything perfectly. Josh had her outside to do her business, and she is ready to go home." She picked up the bag to send home with Ella and added, "I wrote out directions for the antibiotic, and I included a little splitter to make it easy to cut them in half. Keep the cone on her so that she can't get to the stitches." She smiled at the kisses being lavished on Ella's face. "Keep her quiet for the next five days—no running, no jumping, and no stairs."

"I don't do stairs, either," Ella replied.

"And just a couple of bites of soft food tomorrow to be sure that she can keep everything down. Then follow the directions for soft food for the rest of the week. I'll call and check on her tomorrow."

Ella reached out with one arm and grasped Amie's hand. "Thank you so much, doctor. You know how much this little girl means to me."

"I do." Amie walked her to the front of the building and carried the bag to her car. "I'll call you tomorrow, but if you have any questions just call my cell number."

The good feeling that had pushed aside all the negatives lasted until Amie reentered the building and found herself face to face with Gena Watkins. Despite preparing herself most of the day for the encounter, it still felt as though a vise was tightening around her innards. She forced a deeper breath and made eye contact.

"Your bill for Ella McCormick indicated two separate procedures this morning. Is that accurate?"

"Yes, it is. The growth was a minor procedure easily removed while the dog was under for a tooth extraction." In her peripheral view Amie saw Ted approaching and continued her explanation. "Both the pet and the owner are elderly, and I—"

"Decided to disregard policy, even after being warned of consequences. And this is the second time you have released an animal when protocol is to keep them overnight."

Ted, now standing next to Amie, interjected, "I consulted on that surgery and I agree with Amie's decision."

"It doesn't matter whether you agree or not," Gena

replied. "Company policies are not negotiable." She directed her next words at Amie, "I'm sorry that you don't find it important to follow the policies of this hospital." And then the words that Amie knew were inevitable. "We will no longer be needing your services. Your severance will be mailed—"

"Then you will need to mail mine out as well," Ted said, handing her an envelope. "My resignation," he explained.

Gena, who had been delighting in smugness, blanched. She clearly hadn't expected Ted's move. It looked as though whatever comeback she had prepared for Amie was no longer satisfactory.

"You know," Ted said to Amie, "I think I'll stop at Westside for a drink. You want to join me?"

"Yes," she said, "I think I will."

It wasn't until they were facing each other over a drink at a tall table that Amie asked, "So now what?"

"For me?" he replied. "There are other hospitals and clinics. I'll get my resume out there and see what happens. I called Liz and told her. She knew that if you and Ernie both left that I would, too. What about you?"

Amie nodded. "I called Jada. She was aware that this could happen. Her first thought is that I should fight it, but I know that's not feasible. So, it's resume time for me, too."

"Meanwhile," he said and sipped from his beer. It wasn't a question; it was pondering.

"Yeah, well, meanwhile." A sly smile emerged, and Amie explained, "Meanwhile I will revel in the look on Gena's face when you resigned. It truly was priceless. But," she said with emphasis, "why didn't you make her fire you?"

"Liz says it's my maleness. And Liz would make a better Dr. Phil than Dr. Phil. She's right. I wanted it to be my decision, I wanted to choose when to tell her."

"And you wanted to see her react just the way she did."

186

"Yeah," he said with a cocky smile, "there was that."

Amie clinked her glass against Ted's beer. "Thank you for putting a smile at the end of my firing."

"My pleasure."

"And I *do* understand wanting to have control. In a way I did, too. I could have complied with their policies—"

Ted shook his head. "No, you couldn't. But Gena Watkins didn't know that—not for sure. She's really not a good judge of people."

"No, but that's not what she's there for."

"And that's not our problem anymore."

Amie finished her drink and stared at the empty glass.

"Another drink?" Ted asked.

"No. It just hit me that I've got nowhere to go tomorrow—nowhere official, important." She looked up to make eye contact. "What are you going to do tomorrow?"

Ted pushed against the short back of his chair. He thought for a moment, staring into Amie's eyes. "You know," he said finally, "I'm going to go with Liz and my daughter and register people to vote. *That's* important."

Chapter Twenty-Three

It was almost like going to work. Each day after breakfast with Jada, Amie drove to Dusty's. She checked all the animals that were on any kind of medication, and examined any new rescues. It felt good to stay busy, to do what she could to help.

"I couldn't be more pleased with Brandy's progress." Amie knelt to rub the dog's neck, and Brandy moved forward to rest her head on Amie's shoulder.

"She wants a hug," Dusty explained.

"Oh, yes," Amie said, wrapping her arms around Brandy's neck. "I'll bet she gets a lot of these."

"I wish we could give her enough hugs to make up for what happened to her."

Another hug and a kiss to the dog's head and Amie stood. "It makes my heart happy that she's doing so well."

As they left Brandy to socialize with the others in the dog yard, Dusty asked, "What about you, Amie? How are you doing?"

They walked slowly back toward the house. "Surprisingly better than I imagined. When I first started realizing that I could very well be fired, I started going through a mix of emotions. Denial at first—I know that I'm a good doctor, I'm respected and work well with my colleagues, I am dedicated to my work, I spend extra time above and beyond so why would they fire me? Then I got angry at the thought that all of that wouldn't matter, that professionalism and dedication and ability would not be enough. I was left with a decision: could I compromise what I value, what I believe is right and ethical, and do whatever is necessary to keep that job?"

"I'm glad you and the other doctors didn't. It says a lot about what kind of people you are."

"Well, at the moment, we're unemployed people."

"How's Jada handling it?"

"Better," Amie replied. "She was pretty much stuck on anger at the unfairness of it. But I think she is coming around to looking for something better ahead of us."

"Is she going to join us tonight?"

Amie nodded. "Yes, I told her that I was going to help you set up, and asked her to bring soft drinks with her."

"Good. I'm really glad that both of you are going to be here. It's an experience that I've missed being a part of. These kinds of gatherings were common occurrences back in the day. It looks like they are needed now more than ever. I'm no Ali Nichols, but we'll sure do everything we can to get the vote out."

Amie stretched her arm around Dusty's shoulders. "You're Dusty Logan and you're leading the charge for us. That's who you are," she said, stopping in front of a stack of wooden folding chairs on the porch. "Now, where do you want these chairs set up?"

"Come on, I'll show you."

It was a clever use of space. Rows of chairs stretched across the hall through the wide arches, joining the office and the living room.

The gathering wasn't so much a meeting, Amie decided. And it certainly wasn't a rally. The fifty-plus mix from the LGBTQ community brought an enthusiasm and commitment that was contagious. People she knew and people she didn't shared introductions and an energy that was reflected in Dusty's expression.

The energy flushed Dusty's face and took her back years, to a time when a fight for rights felt critical. A time when dreaming of what could be, what should be was more than a challenge to be accepted. It was a challenge with no choices—not for women like Ali and Dusty. They had lived the challenge because to do anything else meant accepting second-class status. It was a time when Dusty couldn't do that. A time like now.

They were all there, members of the community representing the various organizations including Indivisible, MoveOn, and the Town Hall Project. Each brought their diversity, their ideas, and their successes, and shared them with the others. Together their goal was clear. Together they would register more voters than they could alone and bring more first-time voters to the polls of the most important midterm election of their lifetimes.

Each of the organizations presented ideas and strategies, and brainstormed how best to get voters to the polls. They needed to blanket the state, knock on tens of thousands of doors, and have clipboards at malls and churches and all the candidates' events. They needed to have transportation to the polls advertised and available. They needed individual commitments from each member. And if tonight was an indication, they would have it.

Some knew who Dusty Logan was; some did not. But by the end of the evening no one would be able to deny her commitment or her sense of urgency. She saw the need and the possibility and put them together.

"Some of you," Dusty began, looking into the faces that she trusted with a most important mission, "like me, carry invisible scars. They came from resistance against society's handcuffs, from screaming through its gags, and they came from slamming our heads against so many glass ceilings.

191

But we continued to fight because to accept their owner-ship over everything that we knew should be ours was even more painful." She saw the connection in their eyes, the ones who had been there, too, who had fought the same battles. She acknowledged Janine, older and grayer now, a strong advocate and supporter during the push for the ERA. And close by was Brenda, and others who she was sure she recognized but couldn't recall their names. They listened and smiled and nodded.

"And some of you," Dusty continued, "are entering the fray with fresh energy and passion, clear of scars, and just now experiencing painful realizations. Rights, you are finding, are not written in stone. No matter how hard fought the battle to get them, no matter how long we have enjoyed them—they can be gone by the choice of a Supreme Court Justice. By sitting out one election. By assuming the war had been won. That easily, that quickly. Gone." She scanned the young, fresh faces, listening intently, committed to a mission that they never imagined necessary.

"We come from different places," Dusty continued, "dif-ferent religions, different ethnicities, different experiences. But we're here together because we all know that first they came for one of us, and then they came for another. Even-tually they've come for each one of us. And now we know, without doubt, that we are in a fight for our lives, that our world is dangerous, and that we will have to fight like hell to survive. That's why we're here, together, fighting for our collective lives. None of us has ever had a more important mission because by saving ourselves we are saving our democracy." Dusty scanned each of their faces, placed her hand over her heart, and said, "Thank you all for everything that you are about to do."

"And please," Rory's voice projected from the kitchen doorway, "mingle and join us for coffee, soda, and finger food."

Almost immediately the sounds and the atmosphere of the room rose to a social level. It was a positive noise of determination and confidence. It added to Jada's feeling of hope as she joined Rory in the kitchen. "Do you need any help?" she asked.

"You go mingle and get to know your fellow resisters," he replied. "I have plenty of help." He winked and motioned to a man placing a variety of appetizers on a tray.

Jada leaned closer and whispered, "Is that the 'too young, too talented, too handsome for his own good' guy that Dusty told me about?"

"Brandon is too all of that," Rory said with a girlish tilt of his head. "And we're spending way too much time together."

"Maybe that's a good thing."

"Come on. I'll introduce you."

The group had thinned some. Those remaining were engaged in conversations, and Dusty took the opportunity to get a cup of coffee. She stirred in cream as a woman approached.

"Thank you, Dusty," the woman said, "for organizing this. And for igniting what once drove a young warrior to fight for her rights."

"Oh," Dusty replied, "there's so much resistance and energy out there. I just want to do what I can to help harness it. We have to laser focus now on getting out the vote."

"I am so glad to see so many young people here tonight."

"They're essential."

"Yes," she replied thoughtfully, "they are. Oh," she said, soft brown eyes holding Dusty's gaze, "I'm sorry I didn't even introduce myself. I'm Stacy Deakes."

Dusty took the extended hand and smiled. "Thank you for being here tonight, Stacy."

"Hearing you speak so passionately tonight really has

affected me. I understood intellectually and practically how important this election is, but you've ignited the fear and the sense of danger that would come with losing this election."

Dusty nodded. "It's frightening. All that hard-fought progress. That wonderful feeling of normalcy, of freedom to be who you are without even really thinking about it. I had never felt that before—not in its totality, only privately. And now, I'll be damned if I am going to give that up without one hell of a fight."

Stacy's face brightened, animated. She clenched her fist in front of her chest and said, "Yes! Exactly. That's what you made me feel tonight."

The smile that Dusty offered overcame her self-consciousness. She had never imagined herself at the front of a crowd, the one inspiring others. She was, by nature, the encouragement, the support behind, the foundation beneath. Tonight was an anomaly. And it made her smile. Dusty found herself noticing the light dancing in Stacy's soft brown eyes. *Why is it always the eyes?*

"I confess," Stacy said. "I gave up after the sixth circuit voted down marriage equality. I thought we were at the plateau, or even a ceiling, and that we would have to be content with where we were." Her expression had turned pensive. "I felt guilt for that later when the Supreme Court ruled in favor. I'm not about to do that again."

"Since we're confessing," Dusty replied, "it took me a lot longer than that. And it took more than guilt to bring me around—it took a whole lot of anger."

Dusty sipped her coffee. Looking up she realized that Stacy was waiting, holding a cup of coffee, but watching as if she was sure that there was much more to the story. There was, of course, the deeply private, the reasons, the excuses, the desperate lingering sadness. Yes, there was more.

"I lost someone. The one that the fight was for," was all Dusty was willing to give her.

Stacy's brow pressed into concern. "I'm so sorry, Dusty." She placed her hand on Dusty's arm. "My scars don't come anywhere close."

Dusty acknowledged her concern with a nod.

"Which means," Stacy added, "you are more remarkable than I first thought."

The word surprised her. Malala Yousafzai was remarkable. Senator Tammy Duckworth was remarkable. Ali Nichols would have been thought remarkable. Dusty shook her head. "That's not a description I can claim. I think the word that they're using now is 'woke.'" She offered a genuine smile. "I'm woke."

"And, I suspect, too modest. But I don't expect you to claim that, either. What I *hope* you'll do, though, is lead this group to help get out the largest vote Michigan's ever seen."

"That's the goal," Dusty replied. "And with the commitment we saw tonight, it's possible."

Chapter Twenty-Four

2018

Possible, maybe even probable. The goal was front and center, within reach. Weeks of untiring effort from hundreds of volunteers statewide were about to be measured. It was election night at last, the time of do or die, a night that would end in either relief and hope or total devastation. The small group of friends gathered at Dusty's to ride out the night together.

"Here we go," Rory said, as the first returns started coming in. He set a Tums bottle on the end table and settled at the end of the couch with Brandon. "I have no fingernails to gnaw on, so just keep feeding me Tums."

"It's going to be a good night," Brandon said. "Don't worry."

Rory looked into the wide blue eyes and realized that he truly believed that. "You keep telling me that, Handsome."

"I'm with Brandon," Jada added, plopping onto a large pillow in front of the couch and leaning back between Amie's knees. "It's going to be a good night."

Amie wrapped her arms around Jada's shoulders and kissed the side of her head.

"You don't know how much I want to believe that," Dusty said. "And I have bubbly on hand in case you are

197

right. But I'm also well-stocked with the hard stuff if we need to drink ourselves into oblivion."

She began her vigil nestled in the leather recliner, her feet propped comfortably on the footstool. Ninety minutes into the returns, though, she was perched intently on the edge of the seat.

"Shit," Rory exclaimed, dropping his head against the back of the couch. The numbers from Indiana and the other early closings were quickly coming back red. He reached for the Tums. "How many of these can I take in six hours?"

Blue hopes rested in race after race, posting numbers too early or too close to call. Dusty rose and handed the remote to Amie. "My nerves can't take it. Michigan polls are closed now. Check the local station. Anyone else want a drink?"

"I'm with you," Rory said, leaving the couch. "This is the sixteen election on steroids."

Amie flipped the channel, hoping for a bit of early good news. The ticker tape at the bottom of the screen gave updates in each district; then the reports on the major races filled the screen. "Most too early to call," Amie called loud enough to be heard in the kitchen. "One too close to call." No response from the kitchen. "But we're ahead in all of them."

Rory emerged from the hallway. "Seriously?"

"Yes," Amie replied, "and Stabenow and Whitmer by a good margin."

"Come on, Dusty," he said, "you can at least manage to pace."

Pace, yes, she could pace. Down the hall, across the room, to the back of the chair, and back again. She paced through the red seats and stopped behind her chair for yet another "too close to call" announcement. Hours followed of more drinks and doubts, and flares of fears that no matter how hard so many people had worked, no matter what was at stake, nothing would change.

Then, as Brandon left for a bathroom break and Jada turned to a reassuring embrace, the calls began to come in. Blue calls, blue seats. One by one the House number climbed, until finally the magic number.

"Twenty-three," Rory shouted. "Twenty-fucking-three! Oh, God, I can breathe again."

"I told you," Brandon said, still standing, unwilling to break the streak he was watching. "I have good instincts."

Dusty collapsed into the recliner and Jada thrust her fist in the air in victory.

"Come on, Handsome," Rory said, jumping from the couch. "We're serving bubbly, lots of bubbly. It's a celebration!"

"What about Michigan down ballot?" Dusty asked.

Amie switched the channel for the latest results, and the news just kept getting better. When one of the phones on the coffee table rang, Amie picked it up. "Call from Stacy," she announced.

"Oh, it's mine," Dusty said, rising from the chair to claim it. She answered and kept moving into the hall. The excited voice on the other end said, "We did it, Dusty! We did it! Michigan is a female blue wave."

"All the women won? Even Nessel?"

"They haven't called hers yet, but she'll win. And that will make seven, from the governor down. These are smart, serious women. I have a lot of confidence in them."

"And the national results are still coming in. It *is* looking good."

"This is our year, Dusty. This is truly the year of the woman."

"For the first few hours I thought we were living 2016 all over again. I admit I almost gave up emotionally."

"Are we confessing again?" Stacy asked.

Dusty could feel her smile on the other end, and envisioned the light dancing in her eyes. "You seem to have that effect on me."

"Well, in case there's more you need to say, will you have coffee with me tomorrow?"

Dusty smiled. Her cheeks warmed and she replied, "Yes, I'd like that."

They were all waiting, champagne glasses ready when Dusty rejoined them in the living room. Rory handed her a glass and said, "To us, to hope, to two more years of a hell of a lot of work."

They stayed up, stayed the night, and nodded off sometime after four a.m.

At ten o'clock the arousing smells of bacon, coffee, and breakfast brought them to the kitchen. "Ah, my proud warriors," Rory greeted. "Welcome to breakfast a la Brandon."

Brandon turned from the stove with skillet in hand and began dishing omelets onto their plates. "My popular western omelet," he said, "with Canadian bacon, the real thing, on its way."

"You're an angel man," Dusty said, claiming a chair.

"I totally agree," Jada added.

Amie sat down with a smile. "Where were you when I was pulling all-nighters in college?"

Brandon placed a plate of bacon in the middle of the table. "Pulling all-nighters finishing design projects," he replied, "with only fussy clients waiting for me in the morning. My teething period."

"Well, thank you," Dusty said, "for being a blessing this morning."

"And every morning," Rory added with a kiss to Brandon's cheek.

"My pleasure," he replied. "Eat."

▽   ▽   ▽

The girls finished cleaning up the kitchen, then joined Rory and Brandon in the living room.

"Thirty-one House seats and counting," Rory said. "I'm just checking the latest before Brandon heads home and I get to work."

"Will you stay tuned so that you can fill us in?" Dusty asked. "I need to show Amie something."

"You got it," Rory replied.

They retrieved their jackets, hanging in the mudroom, and gained an escort from Sweetie and Rudy who had seemingly inhaled their breakfast. "Did you even taste it?" Dusty asked with affectionate head rubs for both.

"Things to do and places to be," Amie added with a laugh.

"They don't want to miss out on anything, which I have to admit was quite helpful the day of the 'get out the vote' meeting. They brought a lot of attention to adoption." Her tone picked up an edge of excitement. "Two of your kittens and two more dogs found forever homes."

"Now *that*," Amie replied, "is the cherry on top. That makes my heart happy."

"I knew it would."

"Is that what you wanted me to know?"

They walked along the fence of the dog yard toward an outbuilding opposite the barn. "That was part of it," Dusty said. "But I also wanted to ask you some questions."

"Okay."

"I hope you don't think me nosy, but I was wondering if you'd found any good job opportunities."

"There's an opportunity at another corporate hospital," Amie replied, "It's in the Detroit area, though."

"Are you considering it?"

"It might be more of an option than I want it to be. It could come down to how long I'm willing or able to wait for an opportunity at a smaller client-oriented clinic."

Dusty nodded. "Have you ever considered opening your own practice?"

"Oh, maybe a moment or two in that dream state just before you fall asleep. That brief little puff of time when dreams live in possibility."

"Impossible because of cost?"

"Absolutely," Amie replied. "Rent, insurance, cost of equipment and supplies, and even a minimal staff of one. Totally out of reach unless you're independently wealthy or can qualify for a huge loan."

They were standing inside the building where stacks of cans and large bags of dog food lined one wall, and cat food and litter lined another. Amie followed Dusty through a doorway where another room housed boxes of all manner of supplies. And still another room was filled with tools, a workbench and sink, and a second outside entrance.

"Do you need some help with something?" Amie asked.

Dusty was deep in thought, looking around the room. Amie looked around, too, filling the time before Dusty said, "I think there is room at the back of the barn for everything. I think I could even section it off. That would actually make things easier to get to."

"We can help move things whenever you need us."

"Do you think this would be big enough for a vet clinic?"

The look on Amie's face said clearly that she hadn't put the pieces together until this moment. "Are you serious?"

"Too small?" Dusty asked.

"No, I mean are you serious about the idea?"

"Of course I am."

Amie surveyed the building with a new perspective. "I'm sure it would work, but how much would you need for rent? And then there's the matter of equipping it."

"Rent would be big," Dusty replied. "Free care for my animals."

"Oh my God, you're serious."

"Do you think it is too far outside the city for people to come?"

"Not for people who treat their pets as part of their family. I'm more concerned about the cost of equipment like an x-ray machine."

"If you really think that this could work, we can investigate business loans and even, according to Rory, fundraising online." Dusty watched Amie's face, looking for belief in the possibility and seeing the beginnings of it.

Amie's eyes came back to meet Dusty's. "I'm sure I know what Jada will think of the idea. I'm wondering, though, what a couple of unemployed doctors will think."

Chapter Twenty-Five

We're Here Because We're Needed

Dusty stood on the porch, a fresh cup of hot chocolate warming her hands. Last night's snow had been cleared from the drive and paths. Snow and temps below freezing hadn't slowed the transformation. All the supplies and tools had been moved to the barn, insulation and drywall were installed, plumbing done, and propane heat was up and running. The new clinic was almost ready, they were just days from opening, and the scurry of activity was exciting.

A dream was coming true—a dream much bigger than the clinic, with its puffs of possibility breathed so many years ago. It was bigger than Amie could dream, bigger than Dusty thought possible. It came the distance from balding men with the power to brush away the puff of a dream with a dismissive wave of their hand.

Dusty could still feel how the hope for her own dreams had consumed her, how it had held out the possibility of independence and self-confidence. And how, no matter how much she had wanted it, no matter the number of challenges it would have involved, the opportunity to try, to fail or to succeed had been denied her. That denial, she was sure, was more painful than any failure that she might have endured.

But it was long ago, the scars covered by a more excruciating pain—pain that had resisted healing, resisted scarring, that instead had become molecular. It was just part of who she was now. But there had been salves, all along through the years, soothing, comforting, reviving salves. They took many forms—the picture of Ali that she kept next to her bed, eyes so intensely blue, the smile aimed intimately at Dusty. The look, the love was always meant just for her. The picture of the most important part of her life warmed her with cherished memories. And the farm and her animals were salves that soothed her daily. Her home, protective and safe, was occupied by her adopted fur family offering unconditional love and devotion. Here she made a difference, here she was in charge of her life every day. And, of course, Rory, there beside her through it all, year after year, with friendship greater than a brother—or sister. He made her smile and, so many times, laugh out loud. He'd wiped her tears, as she had his, knew her sadness as well as he knew his own. They trusted each other with the best and worst of themselves, and lifted each other up. Life made possible, even enjoyable.

Now as Dusty looked across the drive, she saw a dream coming true—not a personal dream, but one that touched her on so many levels. The clinic was a statement of balance, a chance that she never had but for someone, a shift of power and control. It was real. It was tangible. It was part of a new taste of life, fuller and sweeter than it had been in years.

She left her empty cup on the porch railing and crossed the drive to the new clinic. Amie met her just inside the door with a huge smile and a hug to match. "This is even more than I had dreamed," Amie said releasing her embrace. "Thank you, Dusty."

"It took a collective effort, not just me. The stars lined up for you."

Amie was about to respond when the door opened and

Ted and his wife, Liz, greeted them with warm smiles. "Okay," he said, "We're ready to knock out the last of the painting. Ernie's picking up Josh, and he's on his way. Of course, he couldn't help himself; he's bringing donuts."

"Ha," Amie said, "he's keeping our tradition alive. Jada is on her way, too. She took care of feeding my fur-clan first. She has the website almost ready to go live."

"It's a beautiful thing," Dusty added, "when the stars line up."

"It sure is," Amie replied. "Everyone knows what they're doing and I think I have everything ready for you, but let me know if you need anything else. Ernie's on trim; Ted and Liz are painting; Dusty, you're on outlets and switch covers; and I'm sealing grout. When Rory gets here, Josh can help him unload furniture."

"Okay," Ted said with a clap, "let's go, team."

It *was* a team effort, had been from the beginning—GoFundMe donations and a small-business loan, people working together, laughing together. And a partnership formed where a team of doctors had begun. By afternoon they had dressed the dream in its finest, sleek and professional, tastefully and efficiently adorned.

Josh placed the last of the padded chairs, found at the university resale, in the now waiting room, and the others began to gather.

"Who all are ready to eat?" Ted asked.

"We have enough pizza coming to feed a small army," Amie replied. "I only wish there was more I could do to thank everyone for all your beautiful work."

"Hey," Ernie said, "it's sweat equity for Ted and me. The beauty I see is a partnership that saved me from retirement."

"Amen to that," Ted said with a hand to Ernie's shoulder. He looked at Amie and added, "This team has a lot of good work to do."

"Yes, we do," she returned.

Dusty flicked off the lights behind her and joined the others. "Everyone head on over to the house for pizza and drinks."

"Wait," Rory said, his hand in the air. "First, everyone jump into one of the cars and follow me. Dusty, you're with me."

Rory's truck led them back down the drive to the entrance from the road. He pulled to a stop, jumped from the cab and waved for the others to join him.

Dusty rounded the front of the truck and followed the upraised hand of a beaming Rory. There against the backdrop of early winter's fading light was a large wooden sign framed between wooden posts. In green and black letters, it simply read:

DUSTY ROAD ANIMAL CLINIC.
Drs. Luca, Markum, and Smith
We're Here Because We're Needed

The surprise on her face was expected. The secret had been successfully kept the entire time. Dusty looked into the bright, excited faces, fought off tears, and shook her head. "I don't know what to say."

"You gotta love it! Right?" Jada asked.

Dusty placed her hand over her chest. "I do." She looked from the shining faces back to the sign. She said the words as if she finally had proof. "We did it."

Acknowledgments

"Thank you," whether offered in word or action, sometimes is just not adequate. And recently, that has never been truer. So, as much as possible in the acknowledgment for this book, I offer gratitude and thanks to some pretty special people.

Although it appears that writers often work in a vacuum, we mostly don't. Everyday life takes precedent, demanding our thoughts, our time, and even our bodies. Overtaking the normal impediments this year was surgery. That's when some special people in my life made everyday living tolerable and writing possible. I cannot thank Jo, Jan Payne, Sally Dawson, and Marcy Tyson enough for all they've done to get me through an uncomfortable and frustrating time.

And, without my fantastic Bywater family this book would still be a handwritten manuscript. Thank you to my partners Salem West and Ann McMan for covering their load as well as mine when I couldn't, to editor and typesetter extraordinaire Kelly Smith, copy eyes Elizabeth Andersen, proofing magician Nancy Squires, and media guru Rachel Spangler. Together you have made this possible and I thank you.

About the Author

Marianne K. Martin is the author of twelve novels. She is a five-time Lambda Literary Award finalist, and has taken home one Goldie and two IPPY Awards. She has been honored with the GCLS Trailblazer Award, the Alice B. Medal, and has been inducted into the Saints & Sinners Literary Hall of Fame. Marianne is a retired teacher and coach, and is a founding partner of Bywater Books. Her latest project is a documentary, *The Legacies of Lesbian Literature*, chronicling the impact of lesbian fiction from the 1920s to 2000.

The Liberators
of Willow Run

"An absolutely riveting read from cover to cover, *The Liberators Of Willow Run* clearly showcases author Marianne K. Martin's genuine flair for creating a memorable novel that will linger in the mind and memory long after the book itself has been finished and set back upon the shelf."

—*Midwest Book Review*

The Liberators of Willow Run
by Marianne K. Martin
Print 978-1-61294-079-3
Ebook 978-1-61294-080-9

Bywater
BOOKS

www.bywaterbooks.com

At Bywater Books we love good books about lesbians just like you do, and we're committed to bringing the best of contemporary lesbian writing to our avid readers. Our editorial team is dedicated to finding and developing outstanding writers who create books you won't want to put down.

We sponsor the Bywater Prize for Fiction to help with this quest. Each prizewinner receives $1,000 and publication of their novel. We have already discovered amazing writers like Jill Malone, Sally Bellerose, and Hilary Sloin through the Bywater Prize. Which exciting new writer will we find next?

For more information about Bywater Books and the annual Bywater Prize for Fiction, please visit our website.

www.bywaterbooks.com